A TOWN CALLED TEMPERANCE

F. B. Quick

authorHOUSE®

AuthorHouse™ UK
1663 Liberty Drive
Bloomington, IN 47403 USA
www.authorhouse.co.uk
Phone: UK TFN: 0800 0148641 (Toll Free inside the UK)
*   UK Local: (02) 0369 56322 (+44 20 3695 6322 from outside the UK)*

Published by AuthorHouse   09/21/2022

ISBN: 978-1-6655-9579-7 (sc)
ISBN: 978-1-6655-9578-0 (hc)
ISBN: 978-1-6655-9577-3 (e)

CHAPTER 1

A Rider's Whistle

In the valley between two red rock cliffs, a hundred miles from what could hesitantly be called civilisation, a whistling tune bounces from face to face. At the epicentre of this symphony was a lone figure, shuffling along the desert atop a great black horse. The beast was muscular and mean. It paced across the sands as if it were marching to war. There was a black leather saddle on the monster's back. It was dotted with glistening silver studs; the sun reflected off the studs and formed a pattern of light spots, which followed the figures on the cliffs either side.

In the saddle of the horse was an imposing-looking man in a fine suit, though his clothes were weathered by dust and Arizona skies. An obnoxious whistle bellowed from his lips as he scanned the cliffs that enveloped him. The man swayed gently as the beast stepped beneath him. One hand clenched the reins, and the other flicked and fiddled with a silver switchblade. He winced as the horse changed speeds. This jostled his right shoulder too much for comfort. His nose was bulbous and red, as if it had recently been broken, and he had trouble breathing through it. The top of the right sleeve to his fine pressed suit had a small hole in it. Blood could be seen through the hole, and the area around it was stained red. The man lifted his jacket slightly to peek at a haphazardly bandaged bullet wound; it was still fresh. For such a large man, he seemed awfully tense, although this was perhaps warranted, given his cargo. On the back of his horse was a bloodied and beaten man, with ropes around his ankles and wrists.

The figure on the back of the horse was streaky and thirsty. He silently wheezed, occasionally dodging dirt the monster kicked up into his face. He subtlety groaned as the horse shifted its weight from one side to the other and the bones in the beast's pelvis jabbed him in disparate parts of his torso. This man wore what maybe once could've been called a suit but was now nearly shredded in places, owing to the short period where he'd been dragged behind the beast. His face was covered in shallow cuts, and his right eye was bruised purple from the blunt force of a gun butt. He'd had a slight itch on his nose, which came and went the entire duration of the journey. Occasionally, he'd go to scratch it and remember his hands were bound. Yet this itch was the least of his suffering.

Ropes gnawed away at his wrists and cut into his ankles as he bounced on the horse's back. His scratchy old constraints stripped the skin from his wrists and slowly strangled blood flow to his blue fingertips. His face bounced against the side of the horse's ass, and the force with which his skull bashed against the beast almost left him concussed. One of his boots had fallen off a long time ago, while the other had been eroded down to the point where it no longer fully covered his toes, leaving his feet exposed to the bitter night winds and the scorching sands. His singular remaining black boot had been sanded down to a dusty beige.

The man was about average height, though he seemed skinny and meek in comparison to the man who was transporting him. His name was William Lee and before he had a home, but now he laid on the back of a horse and simmered with pure rage. A loose tooth wobbled and burned in his gum as his head jostled from side to side.

He spattered up some blood from his seeping gum as he attempted to speak. "Where the hell are you takin' me?"

In an almost smug tone, the bounty hunter replied, "I'm takin' you to the nearest town to stand trial, son."

"Stand trial for what?" William replied. He winced as his moving tongue pushed against his sore gums.

The bounty hunter took a long and purposeful breath before saying, "For murder."

"I ain't never mur—" He began to object however stopped to cough as the dust clogged up his windpipe.

And as he choked uncontrollably, the rider simply continued to whistle.

Now the dust was unpleasant, the jolts as the horse moved was manageable, the constant banging of his head was grating, and the itch on his face was infuriating; however, what really brought this unfortunate man's blood to boil was that piercing whistle. After one tune too many, the man finally snapped at his captor and screamed, "Hey, you wanna shut the fuck up! Ain't all this punishment enough?"

The whistling stopped, though it echoed for a moment through the red rock valley. The burly man in the fine black saddle turned to face the man he'd been torturing the past day. He said to him, "For what you've done, buddy, I hope they hang you twice and whistle while they's doin' it!" With that, he spat to the side in disgust.

"I didn't do anything. But I'll still be seein' you in hell, you fat sack a shit!" he replied as he began to chuckle.

The man in the saddle slugged him the back of his head. His cranium bounced off the horse's rear with enough force to knock him unconscious, and he quickly stopped moving, his head slumping down towards the barren floor below.

CHAPTER 2

Road to Damascus

At first, William could see nothing but darkness. He could hear nothing but that irritating whistle and the faint flow of water. He could even feel a bitter easterly wind as it nipped at his exposed feet. Slowly, he managed to heave open his eyelids but only for a short while, as he faded in and out of consciousness.

William watched the ground for what must've been hours, seeing no discernible change in the world around him. The environment was a desolate plain with no features, occasionally broken by a mountain or stream. He had no way of telling time as he drifted in and out of sleep; his only clue as to how long he'd been there was the creeping shadows of dried ferns, which shifted visibly as he rode. However, these plants were few and far between and clearly ambitious to have sucked life from the dry crackling soil. The ground around him walked the line between dirt and rock, with its surface resembling Satan's skin. It was a bleached red with a thousand tiny fissures.

On the occasion the man summoned enough strength to lift his head, he saw sporadic features on the horizon. A dozen rocky stacks rose valiantly in the distance, like giant pillars hoisting up the sky and stopping it from falling on their heads. The relentless sun began to slowly descend over far-off homesteads and rustic ranches. The sky itself was completely clear, save for some rumbling grey clouds, which slowly gathered over distant orange peaks. Piercing shrieks could barely be heard over the rider's whistle. When William looked up, he saw a convoy of vultures tailing the cowboy and his cargo. Looking up expended the last of the man's energy, and he slid back into sleep to the tune of trotting and whistling and storm clouds rumbling.

He finally came to again when he began to feel chilly droplets dot the back of his neck; these droplets became heavier and less sporadic. The sun had long disappeared and given way to a featureless night sky. Everything in the distance was no longer visible, which made the desert feel even more lonely. The rain carried with it a vicious wind, which began to stab at the man's face and his sodden clothes.

The gods seemed to show William some much-needed mercy, as the rider's whistling had stopped. The noise was replaced by a constant dribble of water as it flowed off the brim of his hat and dropped onto his fine leather saddle. The rider had clearly stopped at some point because he now wore a long black tailcoat lined with fur on the inside; this coat was heavy with rain and slapped against the horse's body as they rode. Rain shot downwards at a forty-five-degree angle, beating at the men as they moved through the desert. Great towers of lightning probed the ground, briefly illuminating what was previously invisible.

Maybe it was the wet or the constant motion of the nag, or maybe it was the time he'd spent being dragged behind the horse by his ankles, but his arm restraints sure were feeling awful loose. Yet William knew this wouldn't be enough to escape, as the rider had shown himself more than willing to take him into town with a bullet in each knee. William had no choice but to pray for a miracle to save his disappearing freedom. As thunder struck near and far, the man tried to make conversation with the rider. "How much is they payin' for my scalp—just outta interest?" he asked.

The rider looked at him cautiously for a moment before saying, "More than enough to pay for the rope and the ride. Sheriff McKinley sure does love stringin' up a killer. Helps him sleep at night!" The rider chuckled despicably.

"I ain't killed nobody!" William screamed.

The rider chuckled. "Then it'll be a short trial. Can't say I'm surprised; I been doin' this for nigh on twenty years, and I ain't never had a guilty man on the back of my horse. I've had sobbers and screamers and threateners and bargainers on the back of my horse, and can you believe there weren't a guilty one among 'em... Because I sure as hell can't."

"I ain't like them. You gotta belicve me!" he implored. "Please. I'm innocent!" William begged.

"No, friend, I don't believe you. Hell, I don't believe in innocence! We're all killers, all of us thieves. You just got caught, so take your punishment like a goddamn man and shut the hell up!" he said as a look of satisfaction filled his face.

"Somebody killed my wife, and if you take me to hang, then he walks. What do you think it means for you if you know that and turn me in regardless?" he pleaded.

"I think it means I'll see you in hell, son, you and every other possibly innocent man I've delivered to the noose. But seein' as I ain't in hell yet, I'm gonna enjoy your bounty while I can." the bounty hunter said in a frank and callous tone.

William became desperate in his pleas. "Please, fella, I die tomorrow if you take me in. There ain't no justice in that! Hell, if it's the bounty you're after, I'm sure I have the money to cover it back at my house."

The rider replied, "Now, son, you know my distaste for blubberers and barterers. There ain't a combination of words you could find to make me believe a damn word you say." The rider grinded as he continued. "Even if we turned around, what the hell makes you think I wouldn't just take the money and then deliver you anyway? There just ain't a way out of this for you, boy. You best make your peace with your gods and move on."

William groaned with frustration and dread as he went back to staring at the ground. He noticed they were surrounded by a plateau of jagged stones, cemented into the earth at different angles. Between the triumphant rocky obelisks were a dozen small pockets of razor-sharp scree. The boulders looked like desert fangs, swallowing the men as they trotted down the only path for miles.

The trail they followed snaked between two rising hillsides, covered in these boulders. They followed a thin strip of ground, eroded by two hundred years of passing wagon wheels and horses' hoofs, a trail carved by passing civilisation. The path curved, bent by the largest and most immovable rocks. The men began their slow descent into the valley.

The storm that had seemed to chase them for the past day finally arrived overhead. Above them, huge black masses mingled in great echoing battles, only occasionally illuminated by flashes of thunder. The rumbles and the lightning grew closer, to the point where it scared off the vultures who'd tailed the men for the past ten miles. As the horse cautiously trotted around one of the penultimate twists in the trail, divine justice interfered.

A shaft of lightning slammed into the earth not five feet from the men, causing a smouldering fire among the scree piles. The mighty horse shied in shock, bucking the rider back into the rocks. The riders skull hit a rock as he fell and began oozing blood down its course edge. The blood gently washed away in the rain as quickly as it dribbled out, and the rider lost consciousness before the stream hit the ground.

His cargo tumbled far less violently towards the ground, rolling onto the trail. William immediately began to writhe and squirm in his restraints. The rope around his legs began to slowly loosen as he shifted around in his damp confinements. After what felt like a decade but can't have been more than a half hour, his legs finally slipped free. The apparent outlaw was finally able to clamber to his feet—a dead man, newly walking.

William scanned his environment, looking for some clue as to what had happened. And as his situation sunk in, he triumphantly raised his still bound hands into the air, letting a cold and liberating stream of water wash over him. As the muck and dust ran off him, he ceased his earned rejoicing and dropped back down to the floor. He sifted through one of the scree piles, looking for a piece with a fine enough edge. Finally finding one sharp enough, he placed it edge up between his knees and frantically rubbed the rope along it, splitting each individual fibre until it was weak enough to tear his hands free.

He felt an incredible relief as blood once again flowed unobscured to his colourless fingertips. Standing up, he could see little through the gathering fog and the torrential rain. He knew he had to escape. God had handed him an ace. It was up to him to make it to twenty-one. His priority was finding civilisation—or the closest thing Arizona had to it.

CHAPTER 3

The Land of Second Chances

The cogs in his head began to turn. He considered how exactly he was going to make it out of this desert alive. The first thing he did was limp over to the incapacitated bounty hunter who'd dragged him into this mess. The rider lay face down with his cranium partially opened. His black suit was thick with mucky water, his pressed white collar filled fast with blood. The steady rising and falling of his fat chest showed he was still alive, but when the man placed his hand under the rider's nose, his breath felt shallow and weak. When it became clear he wasn't waking up any time soon, the man slowly eased off his boots and put them on, leaving his own discarded boot on the ground.

As his feet finally found refuge from the rain, he felt a comfort he'd had scant reason to feel since this whole ordeal began. Looking down at the rider, he wondered just what to do with him now. He moved his jacket to the side to reveal a beautiful revolver in his holster. The gun was black steel with an ivory handle, and it had a sheen that only came from neurotic oiling and cleaning. The gun was wrapped in ornate oriental engravings, which snaked around the cylinder and up the barrel. He stashed the gun in his waist before turning to leave but stopped abruptly to empty the man's wallet and take a piece of paper from the rider's breast pocket. The paper was crinkled and soaked with rain. He flattened it over a rock to read it. It was a very poor rendition of his face with the words, "William Lee, wanted dead or alive for horse theft and for repeatedly evading capture.

Has a homestead near Falcon Falls. $45 reward upon his delivery to the Temperance jail."

Not only was this a crime William had never committed, but it also wasn't even the crime for which he was arrested. The bounty hunter was taking William in after discovering him beside the body of his wife, yet clearly somebody wanted him arrested by any means.

William examined the terrible drawing on the poster and began to wonder if it wouldn't be the worst idea for him to head to Temperance. He doubted anyone would be able to identify him from this image, and besides probably being the place he'd find his wife's killer and the man who made the poster, Temperance was about only the town he could reach before he died of dehydration. Maybe it wasn't the best idea to deliver himself to the gallows, but if he didn't find someone to hang in his stead, then his court date would never be more than postponed.

First things first, William needed a way there. He stood up and began squinting through the weather, searching for the beast who'd bucked him. He found the charcoal steed about twenty feet down the road, picking at some dry old grass. He approached it slowly with his hands raised, noticing its breathing as it got louder and deeper. When he was within spitting distance of the stallion, it raised its head and stared down at William. Its salt-and-pepper mane flowed down its neck and draped either side of its ears, which stood open and absorbed every fearful noise William made. Its triumphant legs trotted back and forth slightly.

A shiver strode down William's spine as he contemplated the hole those legs could punch in his abdomen. He inched forward, but the beast jittered slightly with every move he took. Eventually, William simply raised his hand to the white diamond on the beast's face and sat motionless as he waited for the horse to accept him. The stallion finally leaned in and touched his hand, letting William gently stroke it.

The horse, though fonder of William, was still agitated. William reached into its saddlebags and rooted around for something to feed it. This calmed the horse enough for it to be mounted, and though it resisted slightly as William swung his leg over its back, he clamped his feet into the stirrups and clenched his legs tightly around the horse. The beast may not like William, but it would respect him for now. The two began plodding back along the trail—leaving behind some scraps of rope and a bootless cowboy.

William felt a shred of hope as he crested the path out of that godforsaken valley. He'd entered it a man condemned to die and was now leaving it atop a new horse. As he rode, he sifted through the contents of his new saddlebags, searching for what had been taken from him when he was captured. He found his father's watch, a series of letters from his mother in Brandenburg, his old rusty revolver (which he discarded behind him), and a small golden locket with a photo of Abigale. He opened the locket and rubbed his thumb across her face. His hands trembled, and he almost broke down crying.

William felt broken as he looked at all he had left from his old life, but his tears wouldn't stop the hangman, and they wouldn't avenge Abigale. Though the desert was empty and his situation was far from hopeful, the view was far better from up here.

William suddenly came upon the beginning of a steep ridge that the trail cut down. He diverted from the trail and followed the slowly ascending ridgeline, climbing high enough to make out a small town. It burned brightly with the florescent hue of the only street lamps for miles. Temperance, an oasis in the desert.

William studied the looping streets from a distance before continuing along the ridge. Where it slowly descended once more, he found a path running parallel to Temperance. Instead of taking the road in from the north, past the sheriffs' desk and his trusty gallows, William chose to ride into town from the south past the bordello and the saloon. He assumed it would be safer to come in through the wilder side of town.

Riding hard towards the town, William slowed as he got within view to not attract suspicion. The rain died down, and its constant noise was replaced by booming music that emanated from the town. As his gallop slowed to a trot, he passed a splintery old sign that dangled from a frame. The sign read, "Temperance: A Place of Virtue." But one of the chains that suspended it had been shot out, and it dangled awkwardly, one corner just inches from the ground.

William stopped at the Main Street, which was a row of near identical buildings, each painted a more vibrant colour than the last. As he sat in admiration, a dishevelled and elderly undertaker dragged a gunslinger's corpse across the street. William stayed put to let him pass before continuing. He noticed a poster pinned to a dim streetlamp, The poster read, "Vote Waylon McKinley for Sheriff. Bring on a Brighter Tomorrow!" And somebody had graffitied profanity over the top.

It can't have been earlier than one in the morning, yet the residents of Temperance still danced and sung in little pockets of debauchery that reverberated out from the saloon in the centre of town. As he rode, he passed a score of drunken townsfolk and a dozen working girls. William couldn't help but smirk at the chaos of it all.

To William, there seemed no better place for an outlaw to hide than among a sea of them. But he was no ordinary outlaw. He was riding through the town where he was due to be hanged in ripped and ragged clothes atop a stolen horse. William needed a bath and some new clothes to match his fine new boots. Otherwise, he wouldn't be able to hide for long. As William pulled up outside the saloon, he saw the sign offered rooms to let. He dismounted his stolen steed and hitched it up to a post outside. He then took the bounty hunter's money from his saddlebag and began to count it out.

As he climbed the steps to the saloon doors, he was careful to dodge the drunkards who tripped into his path. One patron threw up over the wooden banister not a foot from William's horse, but William simply shrugged it off. He pushed open the saloon doors, and a ghostly figure, formed from the dust this shook off his clothes, escorted him in.

The air was composed of a fine mist of sweat, smoke, and beer. The little oxygen in circulation was thick and overused, having passed through a thousand mouth-breathing barflies. Music echoed from a splintery old piano by the stairs to the lodgings, and each note carried through the stagnant air and rung in the rim of every glass. Half the bar stood or sat in abject misery while the other half danced across tables in defiance of that misery. When the barman wasn't lining up shots for an endless que of desperados and laid-off miners, he was intervening to stop knife fights. A sign hung above the overworked barkeep that said, "Kill a man in my bar, your money's no good here!" Yet part of William was surprised there was a single man left in Temperance who could drink here.

While this was certainly William's kind of place, he was working on borrowed time and couldn't stop to enjoy it. He strode towards the bar and passed varying qualities of men, some of whom were attempting to woo women of the night into a free ride. However, when he leaned over the bar and beckoned the bartender, it fell on deaf ears, as the barman raced to stop a fight that had started at one of the dreary poker tables in the corner.

William couldn't help but smile at this, and he noticed a black feller next to him who also found it amusing. The man couldn't have been older than twenty. There was hardly a hair on his face, and the hair on his head was short and scraggly. He sat with a free stool either side of him—in a saloon packed to capacity—and quickly stooped, smiling when some other folk stared him down from across the bar. The bartender found the two men who'd started the fight and dragged them outside, shouting for them to sort it out themselves. This meant only one thing in the West, and people began clambering to the windows to watch what happened next.

Soon, it was only William and the other man not crowded around the window, and William was finally able to get a word in with the barkeep, asking, "You got a room free, friend?"

"There's 2B, up the stairs and to the right. It's three dollars for you and nine dollars if you'll be wantin' company," the bartender said, growing slightly more hushed towards the end of the sentence yet remaining loud enough to compete with the piano.

"I'll just take the room; you know a place in town that does clothes?" William asked.

"Well, sure. There's a general store across the street. But Mr Perkins don't open till dawn," the barman answered.

"Much obliged," William said as he counted out three dollars from the bounty hunter's money. "How much is your best whiskey?" he asked, figuring he might as well spend this money.

"My only whiskey is a dollar," the barkeep said.

William counted out five dollars and said, "I'll take 2B, a whiskey for me, and one for the fella on my right."

As he threw the money down on the bar, a gunshot bellowed from out in the street, followed by the limp thud of a body hitting the ground. The gawking faces who huddled at the window soon returned to their seats, and their drinking and singing drowned out the sound of the ancient undertaker carting off another corpse. This was justice in the West, and it was no wonder William wouldn't put himself before it.

He asked the bartender, "One more thing." He held out a small bronze room key. "You recognise this key?"

"That's a bordello room key." The bartender said all too quickly. "Don't tell my wife I know that though," he added.

"Thanks, that's all." William replied.

The bartender served the men and placed William's key beside his glass. William downed his drink and then immediately paced upstairs, avoiding all questions and attempted thanks from the man who he'd bought a drink.

As William climbed the stairs to room 2B, the noise grew slightly quieter but no less obnoxious. Though he'd been given a key, he found the door to his room had been kicked off its hinges, so he removed the door and slotted it back in the frame behind him. Though the lack of a lock made him slightly anxious, he knew that lock would do little to stop a posse of lawmen. The room was dingy and dark, only illuminated by a lone oil lamp that burned dimly on the nightstand. The bed was uncomfortable and unmade, its flat straw mattress dotted with suspicious stains. While 2B was far less homely than his bed at home, it was far comfier than the rear end of a horse, so he didn't complain.

He drew a bath but got out quite quickly, as the dirt and sweat from his body formed a mucky broth. After removing his rags and pouring the stones from his boots, William felt free once more. After he'd shaved, he no longer looked like some vagrant vaquero but looked no more reminiscent of his bounty poster. When William collapsed into that bed, despite its uncomfortable feel and questionable history, he slept like a baby.

He was occasionally jilted awake by the feeling of dirt being kicked into his face or the sensation of rope around his ankles. However, the times he was sleeping was the deepest he'd ever slept. He dreamt of Abigale and of his life before all this. For one night, he forgot the sight of her cold body, and the despair it had evoked in him. William forgot just what he was running from and who was chasing him. But he'd remember soon enough.

CHAPTER 4

A New Dawn in a New Town

The discomfort of his bed and the non-stop drinking downstairs woke William not long after dawn. Knowing that time was against him, he quickly slipped on the torn rags he'd arrived in and paced downstairs. As he passed that splintery piano, sticky with booze and stained with dried blood from the previous night, he was stopped by the man he'd bought a drink. He was among the dozen or so people still lingering in the salon. The stranger said, "Well, if it ain't the raggedy cowboy. You shot off before I could thank you proper last night. Unless you got another dollar burnin' a hole in your pocket, I'd say I owe you one," he added in a voice that was awfully coherent for a man who'd spent all night in a saloon.

"I'd love to take you up on that, but sadly, I've gotta get some new clothes," William said in a rushed voice.

"You sure do." the stranger said, looking William up and down with a smirk. "Why you either been bull fightin' or knife fightin'. But either way, you clearly lost."

William smiled but said nothing to the stranger.

The stranger said, "Well whichever one you into, you in the right place."

"Am I now?" William replied, as he threw another dollar on the bar and said, "Get you another one on me."

William turned to walk away, and the stranger shouted after him, "You ever need anything, don't hesitate to ask, cowboy!"

William left his horse tied up outside the saloon and marched across the street, walking as inconspicuously as a man dressed like him could. He walked across to Perkins General Store and said to the man behind the counter, "I need some new clothes, pal."

The shop owner looked him up and down and said, smirking, "Don't you just."

William came out the shop about twenty minutes later with a new pair of jeans, a fancy town shirt, and a fine brown jacket; in the pocket of that jacket was a stack of bills half the size it was when he'd arrived. He now felt less like an outlaw, and the only thing that would make him blend better with the people in Temperance would be a hangover. In fact, William almost felt respectable as he waltzed back over to his stolen horse.

As he unhitched the beast, he moved his valuables to his pockets and put his pistol in his new holster. However, as he looked up, he saw a lifeless and shoeless figure shambling down main street from the north. He saw the imposing stocky frame, the wiry grey hair, and the blood-soaked collar, and he immediately knew who it was.

William glanced around looking for anywhere he could hide. He pointed the horse towards an alley adjacent to the saloon and smacked the beast on the rear. The horse went careening down the alley into one of the towns side streets. William sprinted back up the saloon steps and slammed open the doors, startling the half-unconscious drunks in the saloon. He paced towards the bar and frantically spoke to the stranger he'd seen a few moments ago. "I'm cashin' in that favour; I need to get outta here now," he explained through panicked breaths.

"Woah, friend! Why the rush?" the stranger replied, confused.

"I need a place to lie low, or I'm a dead man. Can you help or not?" William said impatiently.

"OK cowboy. Head out back and turn left. Follow the trail 'till you find and a wooden cabin with a stone wall. You can lay low there 'till nightfall. I'll follow behind ya." The stranger spoke in a calm and collected tone. As William sprinted out the back, the stranger asked, "Who you runnin' from anyway?"

"Some bounty hunter," William answered.

The stranger gulped in fear and said, "Well you best get goin' then!"

William sprinted out the back door and down the trail. The stranger picked up his jacket and hat in as casual a way as he could. As he settled his tab, he mumbled to himself, "Gettin' myself lynched for a glass of whiskey. Ain't that just the way."

The stranger walked out the saloon. As left, he saw a broken and defeated man limping down main street. The bounty hunter's legs almost gave way with each step, and he left a trail of faint bloody footprints in the Arizona sand. He faintly murmured profanity through dry and cracked lips.

The bounty hunter's feet, hands, and face were all horribly sunburnt, and it was clearly agony for him to walk. His exposed feet were mangled and dirt grey, save for the tops, which were tinted salmon pink and freckled. His once fine clothes were faded at the front and dust soaked at the back. The ends of his sleeves and trousers were frayed, and the fibres at the end of his trouser legs were tinged blood red. The thick blood on his collar had dried and solidified in an unnatural position. He limped past the kindly stranger, and when their eyes met, the bounty hunter looked disgusted and ashamed.

The stranger tried hard to hide his joy at the sight of the bounty hunter and simply said, "You OK, Mr Cavanaugh?"

The man gave him a vengeful stair as if this were all his fault and grunted. "Eyes front, boy!"

The strangers' eyes darted to the floor, however he watched Cavanaugh long enough to see him limp into the doctor's office. The stranger walked down the alley to the side street and was shocked to see Butch Cavanaugh's black stallion grazing on the thin strip of grass. The horse took more of a liking to the stranger than it had to William, letting itself be stroked without resistance.

The stranger began to piece together what had happened, and he frantically led the horse to the back of a building two doors down. He subtly knocked on the door and a streaky white man answered, "What time do you call this, Tommy?" he asked in a thick Irish accent.

"Look, Sean, she's all yours if you can run her out of town now!" the man said desperately as he clutched the beast's reins.

"Jesus, Tom, what the hell are you doin' with Cavanaugh's horse?!" Sean said as he snapped awake.

"She ain't Cavanaugh's no more, not if you can take her south without anyone seein'. Can you do it?" Tommy asked.

The man at the door paused for a moment. "Fine. Tie her up out here, and I'll get my coat. Where's Cavanaugh now?"

Tommy replied, "Doctors' surgery. You have some time, but I'd get movin' now."

"I'll get it done," Sean asserted confidently.

The two men nodded to one another, and Tommy tied the beast to Sean's fence. Tommy then continued down the side road, yanking his hat down to obscure his face.

CHAPTER 5

The Wrong Side of Butch Cavanaugh

Following the large cliff that loomed over Temperance town, William walked until it began to descend again. He arrived at a small wooden shack with a waist-high stone wall that ran around the property's perimeter, save for the points that had crumbled long ago. The shack was a rectangular building with low ceilings and sparse windows, and it stood on stilts about two feet off the ground. A few browned and dried ferns dotted the inside of the wall, but they'd finished sucking all the nutrients from this barren soil a long time ago. The strangers house sat just outside the boundary of Temperance and seemed to be built on the driest patch of land for miles.

A small circular patch of grass just outside the wall had been scorched black. The charred spot was just in view of the largest window. It contained a small pile of blackened wood that lightly smoked. William stepped past the wall, and he immediately felt the ground crackle beneath him. He climbed the creaking stairs to the porch, where he passed an ancient rocking chair swaying lightly in the breeze.

The front door was weathered and had a small window either side if it, one of which had been smashed. When he pushed the door open, the wood groaned, and the hinges screamed as it slowly slid ajar. William entered and the floorboards whined beneath his weight; this noise was accompanied by the gentle cracking of shards of glass, which littered the floor. The stranger's home was hardly a home at all but was, instead, a single room divided by a thin wall. Two lamps lit the whole building, one at his kitchen table and one beside his straw mattress.

Though it was daytime, little light was able to enter through the strangling windows. This was worsened by the fact the house sat in the shadow of the cliff. William sat in the only chair, save for the one that gently rocked outside. This lone piece of furniture was parked next to the kitchen table. William laid out on the table all he'd managed to keep from his former life, before realising he'd lost the letters from his mother in all the chaos. He sat in mournful silence, cradling his head in his hands and contemplating what he'd do next.

Not long after, The stranger strode in and threw his hat and jacket on a hook beside the door. He dragged the rickety rocking chair in from outside and sat it across from William, who hadn't even looked up to acknowledge his presence. The stranger slumped into the chair and took a cigarette from his pocket. He held one out in front of William but got no response. "What's ya name, cowboy?" he asked

"William," he replied, still grasping his head in his hands.

"All right, William," He asked as he struck a match, "you feel like telling me how exactly you got on the wrong side of Butch Cavanaugh?"

"Butch Cavanaugh?" William said, confused.

"Yeah! The feller whose horse you rode in on last night. You best start explainin' because I'd quite like to know the reason I'll be murdered!" He said impatiently.

William raised his head, to reveal two light red patches around his eyes. He said, "He was takin' me in for a bounty. Anyway, I managed to escape on his horse, and I made it here. Mr ... uh ..."

"Cavanaugh," He said.

"Yes, Mr Cavanaugh must have followed me here. Or this is just the only place within walkin' distance," William explained.

"So, I'm aidin' an outlaw?" The stranger asked.

"Look, I took his boots and his cash, but I ain't hardly no outlaw! I'm just ... just an opportunist is all," William said desperately.

"If you ain't a criminal, then how'd you end up in Cavanaugh's company?" He asked, sceptically. "Folk don't get picked up by Cavanaugh for opportunism, not white folk anyhow."

"They think I killed my wife." William sighed.

"Did you?" He said, moving back from William slightly.

"No!" William said desperately. "But he found me crouchin' by her body, and I didn't really get the opportunity to explain myself!"

"You really innocent?" The stranger asked. However, he saw the despair and desperation in William's eyes and knew it was the truth. "I'm so sorry about your wife, friend. It's a horrid thing," He consoled, adding, "Bad luck seems to follow you."

"Don't it just. The strangest part is I found a bounty poster on Cavanaugh sayin' I'm a horse thief. Seems like somebody just wanted me gone by any means necessary."

"Ain't that peculiar. You got anyone who'd wanna do you harm?" He asked.

"Not really—at least not now my wife's passed," William replied. "I'm sorry," he added. "I don't think I ever caught your name."

"You made every effort not to catch my name," Tommy said jokingly.

"I suppose I did," William said as he almost smiled. "Sorry about that. I was in a bit of a rush."

"It's OK. It's awful dangerous knowin' me, I'm used to folk not wantin' to. I ain't used to those same people buyin' me drinks though," he said. "My name's Tommy."

"Nice to meet you, Tommy." he replied.

"Well, William, why don't you run me through how exactly you overpowered Cavanaugh. 'Cause you don't exactly strike me as the fightin' type!" Tommy said as he looked at the frail and dejected man who sat before him.

"I ... uh ... He was takin' me in on the back of his horse, and I managed to get out of my restraints and knock him unconscious," William said, lying to reclaim a little of his lost pride.

"Yeah. Cavanaugh's poor knots have saved my ass before as well. How exactly did you knock him out? Don't take this the wrong way, but you and him ain't exactly built the same," Tommy said, thoroughly surprised at what this scrawny man had done.

"I guess you could say I had some divine intervention. I doubt I'd be able to do it again if it came to it though," William said, hiding his shame.

"Well, I'll be damned—Butch Cavanaugh laid out and robbed! I know quite a few people who'd want to shake your hand, William," Tommy said, impressed.

"Not that it matters much, he's bound to find his horse soon anyway. Then he'll scour this town looking for me." William sighed.

Tommy chuckled. "Oh, the horse you so masterfully hid. Don't you worry. I had a friend of mine run it out of town. You should be able to hide out a bit longer."

William looked incredibly relieved. "Really," he said. "You saved my ass more than once then! Look, I owe you a lot more but"—he held out what remained of Cavanaugh's money—"you should take this."

Tommy shook his head and said, "You put me at odds with one of the most dangerous men in this town. If I wanted to get what's owed, then I'd have to take you in myself. Seein' Butch limpin' shoeless down Main Street was about worth it anyhow."

William continued to hold out the money, but Tommy kept refusing it. "You really don't want it?"

"I really don't," Tommy replied.

"Well, it's there if you change your mind," William said as he placed the clip of money on the table.

"Just don't forget it on your way out," Tommy said.

"Who is this bounty hunter anyway?" William inquired.

"He used to run security for a big plantation out East. Even heard him and a few of those other boys used to run down fugitive slaves," Tommy explained. "He moved out to Temperance after the war when business dried up and started scalp collectin' when his buddy was elected sheriff. He usually hauls in a lot more blacks than whites though. I s'pose that's just what he's used to. Looks like he made an exception for you, cowpoke!"

"Lucky me," William said sarcastically.

"You're far from lucky. Cavanaugh's got a lot of sway in this town. He's got a lot of friends in the Klan from his Confederate days, and they've really been gettin' outta hand since those Federal boys went back north. Even the sheriff's not outta Cavanaugh's reach; if the Klan says jump, the sheriff says how high," Tommy said frustratedly.

"So, he's got friends. That ain't enough if he doesn't know I'm even here," William said confidently.

Tommy replied, "It's more than enough. He has most of the town on his side. If it came down to it, there ain't a lawman who'd arrest him, and there ain't a jury with the stones to convict him. You ain't gonna beat him in his own town. As far as he knows you're halfway to Mexico, so I suggest you get at least a quarter of the way there before he decides to follow you."

William shook his head in desperation. "Maybe I could slip back into town at night."

"You ain't hearin' me, Will! That just ain't an option for you. You need to leave, and you need to leave fast!" Tommy exclaimed.

"Let me explain this to you kid. All I had in this whole world was Abigale. And somebody who lives in that town took her from me. So now all I have is the slim chance that I might be able to bring her justice. I just couldn't leave. I won't disappoint her again," William explained as he held back tears.

"Ah," Tommy said as this whole situation began to make sense. He stood up from the rocking chair, walked over to one of his few cupboards, and pulled out a bottle of whisky and two plain glasses. He placed a glass in front of William and half filled it. He then sat down in his seat again and poured one for himself. After he'd finished, he finally said. "How do you know this guy's even there? I doubt he would've stuck around after doin' a thing like that."

William replied, "Why not? He probably knew they was gonna pick me up for it."

"But it ain't worth you pokin' around that death trap for any longer than you gotta; it's a damned suicide mission. You ain't even got the faintest clue where he is!" Tommy exclaimed.

"I got enough to find this prick in a town of fifty people." William said.

"Then why don't ya enlighten me." Tommy said.

William inhaled a deep sigh as he prepared to say something he clearly didn't want to say. "Not long before Abigale died, we got into this big fight. Now it weren't physical, but it weren't civil neither!"

"What about?" Tommy asked.

"I'd been ... distant ... unfaithful. Anyway, we got into this big bust-up about it, and I go down to the lake to let her blow off some steam." A single tear dribbled down William's cheek, followed by another and another. "I hear gunshots not long after, and I hightail it back home." William silently swirled his drink around and looked into his golden reflection in its surface. He continued, "I found this key as I was walkin' up." He threw the key onto the table in front of Tommy.

Tommy asked hesitantly, "What happened, Will?"

He cracked and began balling as his head collapsed into the table. After a few moments of uncontrollable anguish, William finally managed to say, "She was … dead before I got there."

Tommy placed his hand on William's shoulder and attempted to comfort him. "It's OK, William. There's nothing you could've done. You can't blame yourself," he said reassuringly.

After taking time to compose himself, William finally raised his head.

Tommy continued, "What do you know about him?"

William wiped the tears from his eyes and said, "Not, uh … not much, 'sept that he owned that key."

"That's a brothel key," Tommy said as he examined it closer. William smirked through blotchy eyes, and Tommy said, "Hey, fuck you. I'm just tryna help." His tone was joking, and he tried to cheer William up. "And you're sure this isn't Abigale's?" he asked.

William shook his head, saying, "Not a chance. She was from the reservations, so it would've taken a lot for her to come to a place like this—let alone spend the night here."

"Well, it's a lead at least. If, I was you I'd go ask around the bordello for Momma. She'll be able to help." Tommy explained.

"Your momma works at the bordello?" William asked, surprised.

Tommy looked incredibly annoyed at this and warned, "Watch it, cowpoke. She ain't really my momma, but she'll help you if you mention my name."

William said, "Oh OK. Didn't mean to offend you or nothin', kid. Don't take it personal. I really appreciate all you've done for me."

Tommy's anger faded to a smile. "No problem, cowboy."

"Look, you've done enough—more than enough—but would it be OK if I lay low here for a few hours?" William asked politely. "I'd hate to catch Cavanaugh wanderin' about!"

"Sure, I could use the company anyway. But make sure you clear out before sundown, or Cavanaugh will be the least of your worries," Tommy said tensely.

"Why's that?" William asked.

Tommy replied, "Well, uh … men like Cavanaugh take a particular dislikin' to people like me, and this place ain't short on men like Cavanaugh. White hoods are a dime a dozen in Temperance." Worry filled his face.

William finally realised what he meant and said, "They come here in the night?" His voice was filled with disgust.

"Damn near every other night these days. Sometimes it's just rocks and threats. Sometimes I'm lucky to get away with my life. But most nights this week, I've been woken by gunshots and hollerin' as they ride around outside tryna scare me outta town," Tommy said.

"That's horrible!" William exclaimed.

"That's life, cowboy. Hell, I woke up the other night to find a giant crucifix ablaze outside my bedroom window. Damn thing burned so hot the window shattered. I ain't been able to spend the night here since. That's why I was rottin' away at the bar all night. I ain't even a big drinker; least I wasn't before this all started," Tommy explained, slightly terrified thinking about it but happy someone was finally listening to him.

"Jesus Christ, I knew some folk had more hate than sense. But that's a whole nother level. They hate you more then they hate me," William said.

"That's why its best we both clear out before dark. For all we know, Cavanaugh might be under one of those white hoods, and he'll be wantin' his boots back," Tommy said.

"Don't worry, kid. I'll clear off soon. You mind if I borrow a pair of your boots?" William asked. "I'd hate for that to be the reason I got hanged."

"Sure," Tommy said. "Bottom of my wardrobe. But I only have one other pair, so you'll have to leave those for me."

William went to the wardrobe on the other side of that razor-thin wall and pulled out a pair of grazed old boots with holes at their tips. William felt it was a shame to trade his shiny black preachers for these raggedy old things. But fashion was the least of his priorities right now. So they'd have to do. He put them on and returned to the table with Tommy.

"So, Will, whereabouts are you from originally?" Tommy asked.

"I moved here from Philadelphia, but my family's from Germany. My pa was a gambler and a drunk. He used to beat my ma to within an inch of her life and then hand me some coins and make me walk her to the doctors. Eventually when I got old enough, it was my little brother walkin' me to the doctors. One day while my mother was bedridden from the last round of bruisin', he just packed our bags and bundled us on the first boat to the USA. And I never saw my mother again. I never much got on with my old man, and I hated how much my little brother wanted to be him. As soon as I was able, I moved as far from him as I could. I eventually found myself in Arizona, where I met a lovely girl. I wrote to my folks to tell them we were getting married. My father was furious. He was somewhat of a purist. My mother wanted to come out to meet her but … but she passed before she ever got the chance. My father died not long after that."

"I'm sorry to hear that. Do you ever hear from your brother?" Tommy asked.

"I got a letter from my brother about a year ago. He said he was pleased for me; said he'd found a wife of his own and they'd bought a house near Pittsburgh. I'm happy for him. I know he's a good man underneath it all. But he didn't half sound like my father. It's a shame," William said as he sighed.

"Seems we all either become our fathers or actively become the opposite. I think you made the right choice," Tommy said.

"I'm not sure I did. Towards the end, with Abigale I mean, I was cold and closed off. The only way I could've driven us further apart was if I physically moved away like he did. I didn't kill her, but I took her life away, trapped her in a loveless and effortless marriage. Maybe she'd have been better off without me; maybe she'd be alive without me," William said.

"We all make mistakes, William; we all have things we regret. But you have far more to be worried about than torturing yourself. It'll do you no good. and it'll bring her no justice. We just have to try and live for today before it's gone," Tommy consoled.

William attempted to change the subject before he began to cry again. "Where are you from, Tommy?" he asked, his trembling voice almost choking on the words.

"I was born here. Hell, my old man used to live in this house, though we didn't have much choice in the matter," he said.

"Have you always lived in this house then?" William asked.

"No. I lived in town with Momma after my father passed, but I moved back here a few months ago."

"You lived in the bordello?"

"I did," Tommy replied. "I never knew my ma, so Momma was about

28

the only person I had left. She raised me like one of her girls, made sure nobody laid a finger on me."

"Sounds like a tough woman," William said.

"You don't know the half of it," Tommy replied. "I eventually decided I wanted to live on my own, and I moved into my father's old house. I've regretted leavin' ever since. But I just can't move back in with her. I don't think I can burden her with protectin' me forever."

"That's fair enough. I think at some point every man must live and die on his own merits. The things you've been put through are rotten, but that doesn't mean you have to let them stop you from standing on your own two feet," William said.

The two men drank and smoked for hours as they chatted and laughed, almost forgetting all their problems in the meantime. However, as William looked out the window, he realised the sun was beginning to set. He said to Tommy, "I should probably get a move on."

Tommy replied, "I won't be far behind you!"

William said, "I'll find you later if I ain't shot or skinned. Will I find you at the saloon?"

"Either drinkin' there or drinkin' in heaven. I'll save you a seat regardless," Tommy replied.

"You'd better. Pleasure to meet another dead man walkin'," William said as they both laughed.

Tommy laughed some more as he collected up the glasses and took them over to his sink. As his back was turned, William swiped the whisky bottle for the road and left the stack of cash in its place. Before Tommy could insist he take his money back, William had picked up his coat and was heading for the door.

"Don't be a stranger, cowboy!" Tommy shouted after him.

"I think if Temperance had a few more strangers like me, folk wouldn't get shot so much." William chuckled to himself as he left.

CHAPTER 6

Returning the Favour

William paced out of Tommy's house, pulling his jacket collar up to obscure his face and swinging the bottle of whisky by his side. The sun had barely half crested the horizon, so he decided to wait until night to go back into town. Instead of heading back towards Temperance, he turned around and walked up the slope that led up the cliff. He slowly ascended until he could see Temperance from end to end in the distance. He came across a fallen and rotting log, next to the stump that the winds had ripped it from. He rested on in and it flexed beneath his weight.

William placed his whisky by his feet and stared down the near sheer drop to the trail below. His eyes eventually drifted up as his gaze followed that winding path that snaked through Temperance and diverged into every rotten back alley. He kept his right hand free to take the occasional swig from the bottle, while his left hand remained in his pocket clutching his few possessions.

Maybe he'd become numbed to passing time on the back of that horse, but he could've sworn the sun sunk beneath the horizon far more quickly than he was used to. Soon the only light for miles was the fast-dying twilight from the setting sun and the faint streetlamps of Temperance.

As William smoked and sipped on the ridge, he could see Temperance splitting into two separate towns. The north side was calm and quiet, perhaps kept in line by their view of the gallows. The south side came alive at night as dozens took to the streets to drink and brawl and whore till dawn. From his vantage point, he could see all down Main Street until the streetlamps dwindled across town.

On the north side of town, where there wasn't a party or drunkard to be found, William could clearly make out gathering torches outside the sheriff's office. The torches clumped together and circled for a moment, and the five faint lights began to move down Main Street. Trouble was brewing on the other side of town.

The torches moved in a loose formation, travelling at a stepping pace as they traversed the the south side of town. They diverted down a side street, and they suddenly sped to a canter and then to a strident gallop. The pack of lights accelerated and began to illuminate a thick cone of dust, kicked up by the stallions. Their torches obscured the riders and their horses, with only the glimmer of light from their steel stirrups and saddles to show they were men on horseback.

Over the still audible tune of the saloon piano, William could faintly make out the noise of men as they cheered and hollered. They passed turn after turn and made no attempt at slowing. Their hazy silhouettes became clearer as they drew closer. William filled with horror as he squinted to try and distinguish faces and saw only blank white hoods. The five torches passed the last turn onto main street, and it dawned on William where they were heading.

He stood up and turned around to see Tommy leaving his house and walking back towards town, unaware of the riders coming his way. As they passed his hilltop vantage, William raised his pistol and contemplated firing on the column. However, he instead began heaving the great dried log to the cliff edge. The log was lighter than expected, as it was cooked free of any moisture. However, it was made harder to move by the fact it nearly disintegrated as he pushed it into line with the precipice.

When Tommy finally saw the riders come into view, he desperately turned and tried to run back to his house. But before he could jump through the hole in his stone wall, the riders circled him and blocked his path.

The Klansmen fired gunshots into the air and beside his feet. They took intense pleasure in cackling as Tommy jumped to avoid the whizzing bullets. One of the riders swung a lasso around Tommy's neck and yanked it tight as it clamped around his throat. They began to drag him back to

Temperance to the tune of jeers and applause. Tommy could do little but squirm and writhe as he desperately tried to suck what oxygen he could through his fast-collapsing windpipe.

William poured his whisky all over the log and crouched behind it, watching in horror as they dragged Tommy towards Temperance. He peered down the cliff and waited for the riders to come into the log's path. When they got close enough, he lit it ablaze and shoved it over the edge. Fire quickly consumed the log as it tumbled towards the ground. William ducked to the floor, peeking over the edge at the rolling tree trunk. The flaming log went careening towards the men.

When the first two horses caught sight of the log, they panicked and reared up, flinging the men from their backs. The log rolled through the front of the column, colliding into those horses who hadn't immediately run. Two of the horses carried their riders far out into the desert, while the others all bucked in panic and threw their riders into the dirt. The rider who'd roped Tommy was thrown far back into the sands, as he'd chosen to clutch Tommy's noose instead of his reins. His hood tumbled off as he rolled to a halt, revealing the sweaty oaf beneath it. The man finally let go of Tommy's rope as he realised his face was on show, searching for his lost hood.

Three Klansman remained at the foot of the cliff. One clutched a red patch on his hood as the gash beneath it bled. The other desperately sifted through the desert sand as he looked for his hood. The final Klansmen was balled up in the foetal position behind a nearby rock.

Tommy forced his hands into the space between his neck and the rope and frantically gasped for air. And as one of the Klansmen went to pick up the rope once more, William stood up on the ridge and fired a shot at the earth by his feet. the Klansman dropped the rope as a tremendous bang swept over the area like a tsunami of sound. One of the Klansmen immediately began crawling away, but as the other two stayed put and scanned the clifftop. William fired two more shot at them. William would never be able to land a shot from this distance, but the remaining Klansmen got the message. One of them helped their wounded comrade to his feet before limping into the black desert.

Tommy finally ripped the rope from his neck, and for a few seconds, he just lay on his back gasping for air. Once the shock had passed and his trachea had returned to its normal shape, he slowly got to his feet and looked around for some clue as to what had happened. Not knowing quite what to make of this, he looked up to see a distant figure waving on the cliff's edge before disappearing into the darkness.

Tommy was terrified as he saw another figure riding up the path on a fine white horse. He initially turned to run, but the light from the burning log and the scattered torches bounced off the star on the stranger's chest. As the man trotted towards Tommy, his fine white horse came into view, its pink nose still panting from the ride. On the horse's back, the man's features could be made out. He was heavyset but hardly fat, and he had pale blue eyes that darted about in his head and contrasted with his pasty skin. A ten-gallon hat sat on his head, and thin grey hairs cascaded down around his cauliflower ears. He had a bushy salt-and-pepper moustache that wriggled as he chewed a toothpick. The man had an imperious air about him, and he always seemed to be looking down on Tommy. In one hand, he clutched his horse's reins, while the other hovered above his side iron. His eyes scanned around for any clue as to what had happened here, until his piercing gaze eventually landed on the man at the centre of it all, Tommy.

Tommy could faintly make out a figure descending the far side of the cliff, but he quickly averted his eyes to not alert the law to who was almost certainly William. The sheriff's horse trotted to a stop as he marvelled at the scene in front of him. He furrowed his brow as he contemplated what to make of all the carnage and the gunshots and the still burning log. The log began to smoulder, and it produced a thick fog of smoke that hung in the still air.

Amid this apparent chaos, amid strewn weapons and discarded torches was Tommy, still gasping for breath and cradling the rope burns around his neck. The sheriff saw two fleeing horsemen as they turned towards Temperance. He simply chuckled to himself and said, "So, you gonna tell me this ain't what it looks like?" The sheriff spoke in a deep and raspy voice, and on the twinge of certain words, you could hear the rye whisky and cigar smoke as it echoed off his tonsils.

Tommy's now wheezy voice was a good octave deeper than before. He slowly choked on the words as he said, "No, sheriff. I'm afraid this is … exactly what it looks like."

The sheriff pulled a handkerchief from his pocket and coughed out some thick smoke. He then asked, "You wanna continue this conversation somewhere else?"

Tommy nodded as he turned around to walk back to his house.

The sheriff shouted after him, "I meant the station, son!"

"Awful long walk just to get hanged again," Tommy wheezed.

As he turned to walk away once more, he enjoyed the taste of the crisp and fresh air. Though it may well soon be snatched away from him, for a moment he enjoyed the sensation of breathing free. Tommy stumbled up the steps to his house while the sheriff impatiently followed him and tied up his horse.

Tommy shoved open his door and fell into a chair, moving the clip of money William had left into his pocket. Tommy couldn't decide whether to fall asleep or break down crying, but he decided to do neither as the sheriff followed him in. The sheriff looked around Tommy's shack, and a look of disgust filled his face for a moment. He scowled as he stepped across the pile of broken glass. However, he soon realised how exactly it had been broken when he caught a glimpse of the charred wood outside the window. The sheriff pulled out a chair with his handkerchief and sat across from Tommy.

"What happened, son?" the sheriff said, sounding far more empathetic than the tone he'd used initially.

Tommy's voice, though still strained, finally returned to normal as his trachea began to regain its shape. "What? You didn't get reports of that?" He sighed painfully as he continued. "Who would've reported it? Justice is blind in Temperance I suppose." He chuckled nihilistically.

"Son, I know you been through a lot, and I know things have been rough in the past, but I can help you if you let me," the sheriff said defensively. "Help me bring you justice—"

Tommy interrupted, "Things are still rough, sheriff! Is this what justice looks like to you?"

McKinley averted his gaze.

"Look!" Tommy shouted as he pointed at the rope burns on his neck. "There ain't no justice here—not for me at least."

"This ain't what Temperance is, son," the sheriff implored.

"Ain't it? Where was your deputy tonight then, sheriff? I bet he was under one of those hoods."

The sheriff tried to interrupt.

But Tommy just carried on. "I've seen the way those people look at me. I've even seen the way you look at me when nobody's watchin'. There ain't no justice for me in this world. But your justice is comin' in the next."

"It don't have to be that way." the sheriff exclaimed.

"But it is. I appreciate yo efforts, phoney as we both know they are. But those boys will be back tomorrow, and the day after. If you really want to help, you can either do your damned job"—Tommy slowly exhaled before continuing—"or you can cut me down and bury me when they're done. Now if we're done here, get the fuck outta my house!" Tommy gestured to the door before laying his head on the table.

"OK son, if that's what you want," Sheriff McKinley said as he got up from his chair. "Get a cold flannel on that rope burn. Don't let them catch you alone!"

Tommy said nothing, having no more words for the likes of him.

After the sheriff had gone, Tommy began sobbing uncontrollably to himself. He grabbed a new bottle of whisky from under the sink, and his shaky hands poured out a glass. The tears streamed down his cheeks and cut trails into the dust that covered his face. His shirt was ripped, and his once black trousers were now a thick and dirty brown. His boots, which were already covered in loose threads and sporadic holes, were now completely ruined, and the sole of one of them had been completely torn off.

Tommy wept uncontrollably for the next hour, the only times he stopped being when someone rode past outside, which caused his heart rate to crescendo and his eyes to dart around. He reached a point of strange clarity, where he had no more tears left to cry, no more energy left to expend, no more fear left to feel. This was also around the time he ran out of whisky, so he cleaned himself up a bit and got ready to head to the saloon.

Tommy collected a rusty old revolver from under his sink and concealed it in his waist. He slipped on the last pair of shoes he had, which happened to be Cavanaugh's boots, and covered the rope burns on his neck with a red bandana.

Tommy left for town, glancing over his shoulder almost constantly, watching for shapes in the desert the entire way there. Tommy was understandably jumpy, and the mere sound of hooves was enough to startle him into reaching for his gun.

Fortunately, the few people who rode past Tommy on the way to Temperance took little notice of him. That brief walk back to town was among the longest walks of Tommy's life. He'd made it out alive, but he was on borrowed time.

CHAPTER 7

Momma Knows Best

William slinked across the top of the cliff and slowly descended the other side, blending in with the desert shadows as best he could. Eventually, he reached the northern road to Temperance and began to walk back towards that place. He veered right off the trail, not wanting to stroll past the sheriff's office, and eventually found the other end of that back road he'd run down this morning. He worked his way down the side roads that flanked the town, ducking into alleys whenever he heard faint murmuring or approaching hooves.

William caught a glimpse of the lights that beamed on main street, his eyes slowly adjusting after spending so long squinting at distant torches. He followed the noise of the triumphant piano and soaring singing to the saloon, which bounced with life like any other night.

Sneaking down the alley adjacent to the saloon, sticking to the walls, he surveyed Main Street to check the coast was clear; he saw the faint glint of a star as he peeked out. He immediately turned around and bent over, pretending to throw up. This worked, and the sheriff didn't even look twice in his direction. The sheriff trotted down Main Street, looking disdainfully at his constituents.

Once the sheriff had gone, William ducked across the street and walked towards the bordello. He climbed the steps and felt an incredible relief. There were no lawmen here, at least none on duty. The scent of sweat and God knows what else wafted over him as he opened the door.

The walls were a deep red, and two were covered by a red curtain with golden tassels reaching down to the floor. The other two walls were adorned in all manner of erotic art, the frames of which were gold as well. A great chandelier dangled in the centre of an ornately patterned white ceiling. The chandelier, too, appeared all gold, save for the wicks and the wax. The floors were thick ebony hardwood and were surprisingly clean. Sparse red and gold furniture dotted the room and got more common as you approached the bar. The bar itself was an imposing slab of ebony, covered with a floral pattern that converged into some sort of crest in the centre. In front of the bar were some red velvet bar stools and behind it was a pretty blonde in a too-tight corset. To the left of the bar was a grand piano and a small figure hunched over it, tapping out slow and calming tunes that kept the room docile.

One of the curtains was held open by a golden rope, and it revealed an ornate staircase, flanked by a golden banister. A dozen working girls shifted across the room, picking up drunks and leading them upstairs. Some of these girls came up to William, but he kept his gaze to himself, for perhaps his first time in that establishment.

The other men in there were truly a cross section of society. Half were slobbering gunslingers who'd come in from across the street, and the other half were stern-faced folks who seemed eager not be recognised by anyone. All these men were going to the same place eventually—up that golden staircase to relieve their urges and part with their riches.

Two women went to strike up a conversation with William, and he declined them both, talking instead to the blonde in the blue corset behind the bar.

The woman behind the bar asked, "Can I help you, sir?" her eyelashes fluttering as she spoke.

"Maybe you can. What's you name mam?" William asked.

"Tilly," the girl said hesitantly, unaccustomed to men speaking to her so formally.

"Well, Tilly, I'm lookin' for a woman named Momma. I'm hopin' you could point me in the right direction," William said.

Tilly immediately stopped fluttering her eyes and puffing out her chest. "What exactly you want with Momma?" she said suspiciously.

"I want her help; I think she can point me to the man who killed my wife," William replied in a slightly hushed tone.

The woman's voice became slightly more sympathetic, but she remained equally suspicious as she said, "Well I'm sorry for ya loss," adding, "What if Momma don't wanna speak to you?"

"Then tell her Tommy sent me," William said.

Tilly's eyes lit up as she heard Tommy's name.

He continued, "If that don't convince her to see me, then I'll get up and leave. Momma don't sound like the kinda lady I'd want to cross."

"She really ain't." Tilly said. "Look I'll ask her, but you should know, outsider, folk what cross Momma usually end up as pig feed." her tone becoming more threatening.

Tilly told another girl to work the bar and then disappeared behind one of the curtains. The last thing she said sent a shiver down William's spine, and he couldn't help but wonder who exactly he was asking after. He wasn't left to wonder for long, as, after a few moments of mumbling from behind the curtain, the bartender emerged. She held the curtain open and gestured towards a door behind it. William stepped through the door and heard the curtain swish closed behind him.

He entered a deep office with a towering ceiling. The whole room was decorated with wood carvings, and the walls on either side were covered by imposing bookshelves full of the great works of human history. On the back wall was a large semicircular window of stained glass that stared out onto Main Street.

He closed the door behind him, and this, combined with the curtain draping shut, muffled all noise coming from the bordello floor. This was perhaps the only quiet place in Temperance, save for the gallows on hanging day.

In the centre of this beautiful office sat a gaunt-looking woman, no younger than sixty. Though her skin was wrinkled and aged, her eyes were as sharp as ever, and she'd already sized William up before the door clicked shut. Her hair was grey, but still looked healthy. She poured over papers, ignoring William save for an initial scanning glance.

He coughed to get her attention, but she didn't even flinch. She just gestured at the chair in front of her with the end of her pen. William sat in the chair patiently, looking over the volumes of her shelves for any words he could actually read. It became clear to him, even before she permitted the conversation to begin, that she was an intelligent woman—especially in comparison to the rest of Temperance.

After several moments of tense silence, the woman lifted her head and looked at William. He could tell from her look that Momma didn't think much of him. She said, "So stranger, why does Tommy think you're worth my time?"

"Somebody killed my wife," he said, almost choking on the words as he spoke.

"Maybe you misheard me because that ain't what I asked. Why does Tommy think you're worth my time?" she said confidently as she leant back in her large leather chair.

William hesitantly said, "Well, ma'am—"

"Momma," she interrupted.

"Right. Well, Momma, Tommy thinks I didn't kill her. And he seems to think you can help me find the man what did. I guess Tommy don't think it's just for me to die for a crime I didn't commit," William said in a remarkably composed way given that they both knew he was begging.

"Well, Tommy's a good kid, but he's real sentimental, and look where that's gotten him. So besides altruism, why do you think you're worth my time?" Momma said in a cynical tone.

William thought for a moment, realising that further grovelling would get him nowhere. "Somebody in your town's got a pension for killin' innocent women, Momma. I'd say it's in your interests to help me find this person before they put one of your employees in the ground," he said, slightly more confident with his argument.

She smirked to herself and said, "Employees? We're under no delusions here, sir. You can call them what they are. What's your name, mister?"

"William ...Roberts," he added cautiously.

Momma grinned to herself once more. She unlocked her desk drawer and slid it open to reveal a stack of papers weighted down by a silver six-gun. While William's eyes were fixed on the gun, Momma glanced at the piece of paper below it before pushing the draw shut. She never relocked the drawer, and William noticed she never let her hand stray too far from it. She said, "Why is it you came to me, Mr Roberts? If I were trackin' a killer, then I might reasonably go to the sheriff."

William seized up slightly when she mentioned the sheriff but quickly answered, "I don't think the sheriff can tell me whose key this is." He placed the key on the desk in front of Momma.

"Right," Momma replied. "Well, I can tell you that's one of my keys."

"Can you tell me whose it was?" William asked frantically.

"Perhaps. But as we've established, I don't conduct business on the basis of altruism Mr Roberts," she replied in a slow tone, which contrasted William's.

"I could pay you for your help," he proclaimed, not knowing exactly how he was going to follow up on this.

"Look around you, Mr Roberts. I have money. What I don't have is the liberty to move in this town without the law crawlin' up my ass. Now since you're the kinda fella who strives for justice in this cold and unfeelin' world, maybe we can work out some kinda arrangement," she said, sizing him up once more.

"What exactly are you sayin'? Because I'm no hired killer if that's what you're implyin'!" William said angrily.

"Really. Out of curiosity is it the killer part or the hired part to which you're objectin'?" Momma asked calmly.

"The killer part mostly!" William shouted

"Lower your fucking voice!" she said firmly as her hand drifted to her drawer. "What was you plannin' on doin' when you caught your wife's killer? We both know you weren't going to take him to the sheriff," Momma said.

William was too distracted by his anger to really listen to what Momma was saying. She continued in the same collected tone, "Look, son, a week ago you were a happily married man. People gotta adapt sometimes. You think those girls out there want to do what they do? They're just doin' what they have to; they're survivin'." She paused afterwards to let William calm down for a moment.

William's heartbeat slowly fell as he pondered his options and rubbed the locket under the desk. He'd come too far to give himself to the noose now. He cautiously replied, "Who is he?"

"Is that a yes?" Momma asked.

"It's what it sounds like. Who is he?" William said.

"Last night, some real piece of work comes stumbling through the doors, carryin' a bottle and some pieces of paper stamped with red ink—looked like a foreclosure order or somethin'. He spoke in this slurred Southern twang, which made my black girls give him a wide berth, and before long he was chattin' to one of the other girls. Men like him are good for business because the brown usually puts them on their backs before long, but sometimes they just bring trouble. Anyway, he starts chattin' to this girl called Lucy, sweetest girls you've ever met. I mean she got eyes like a goddamn puppy dog—far too sweet for this line of work." She stared down with sadness as she continued. "So, he follows Lucy upstairs, grippin' her hips a little too hard. About ten minutes later, I hear an ungodly crash, followed by Lucy screamin', and then Tilly bursts through my door and tells me he's sat on her fuckin' chest, chokin' the life from the from the poor girl."

William looked appalled as Momma kept speaking, "I'd already grabbed my gun when I heard the first crash, and I bound upstairs and started poundin' on the door. I look through the peephole and see this fat fuck hunched over her, squashin' her windpipe with one hand, strikin' her with the other! I move my girls back from the door, and I start bootin' the thing. When it doesn't budge, I raise my revolver to the lock and pull the trigger. The scorchin' hot lock pings off, and I boot the fucker open. But by the time I got in he'd already ran out onto the balcony. He jumps off and sprints across the road, and I fire two shots at him as he runs; one strikes the dirt, and the other hits the guy in his right leg." She paused for a moment, clearly distraught before continuing. "He gave Lucy a broken jaw, three cracked ribs, and damn near killed her, and I couldn't make a kill shot from ten fuckin' feet away!" Momma sounded furious with herself as she finished speaking.

William was speechless for a few moments and soon said, "Look, not that it don't sound like he's got it comin', but I've got enough problems in this town already!"

"I'm well aware of your problems, Mr Lee, as poor as that drawin' of you is." Momma replied frankly.

William's face dropped as he realised Momma knew who he was. He stuttered, "You ... you know my—"

"Yes," Momma said. "And if I believed any of your posters then you'd already be dead," she added as she slid her draw open once more.

William sat in stunned silence as Momma continued.

"As much as empathy is not a helpful trait in my business, I like to think I operate based on a moral code of sorts. I'm not blackmailin' you, Mr Lee. If you want to leave here without my help and continue your virtuous crusade on your own, then I won't tell a soul. But if you want my help, I'm going to need yours. And we can make this world a better place together."

William replied, "That's a great sentiment, Momma. But I'm a wanted man. What if Cavanaugh finds me while I'm runnin' yo errands?"

"Why he'd cut ya ball off and hang you twice for good measure. But lucky for you, Cavanaugh's outta town tonight, traipsin' through the desert lookin' for some clue as to where you went," Momma replied.

William finally relented, seeing no other route to his goals. "Fine," he said. "I'll do it. Where can I find him?"

Momma smiled and said, "At the saloon, no doubt. It's the only bar in town that won't shoot him on sight. His name's Marcus Thompson. Tommy should be able to point you in his direction. Hell, the kid'll probably thank you for it."

William replied, "Maybe, but it don't seem like Tommy's thanks carry's a lot of weight in this town."

"It does in here," Momma replied. "It's about the only reason I let you near my door. Anyway, I'd say a man in your position needs all the friends he can get!"

"How do ... er ... how do you want me to do it?" William asked, lowering his volume.

"In an ideal world, slowly and painfully. But quietly is probably best. Once you're done you can lay low here for as long as you need," Momma said.

William nodded sombrely as he stood up to leave.

As he left Momma said, "I look after my girls because they're just tryin' to survive in world that doesn't want 'em. You have that in common."

William listened over his shoulder as walked out. He opened the door and turned to the old woman. "Sure sounds like altruism to me."

And with this, he left into the night, delivering justice to one man so he could deliver it to another.

CHAPTER 8

The Murder of Marcus Thompson

After a few moments of looking around, William finally plucked up the courage to cross main street once more. He followed the sound of music and the scent of fresh sick to the saloon, moving from shadow to shadow and occasionally ducking into packs of drunks to avoid being noticed. When he reached the base of the steps, he waited for a group of patrons to stumble by and snuck in behind them. William saw Tommy at the bar and went to sit beside him. Tommy was hunched in a stool with a red bandana around his neck. He initially jumped when he saw movement in his peripheral vision. However, when he saw it was William, his face lit up. He said, "Well, cowboy, I'd say I owe you a drink—unless you got another lynchin' to stop that is!" He patted William on the arm, adding sincerely, "Listen, William, I really am thankful. There ain't many folks who'd stick their necks out like that for me. It's just nice to know someone thinks I'm worth savin'."

William had initially not focussed on what Tommy was saying, instead glancing around the bar looking for his target. But when he heard Tommy say this, he gave him a warm look. "Come on, kid. You don't gotta thank me for anythin'. It ain't your fault this whole town's rotten. Besides, you won't have to wait long to repay me. My head'll be in a noose soon, no doubt." William smiled.

Tommy changed the subject, partially to stop himself from bursting into tears. "Since you ain't workin' your way through a pig, I'm guessin' Momma heard you out."

William went back to scanning the bar, "I guess she did in a way, and I'm guessin' mentionin' you had a lot to do with that. She said ..." William stopped for a moment before continuing at a hushed volume. "She said I gotta kill someone for her"

"Jesus, cowboy, it ain't the best of situations you've gotten into. You're killin' folk to find folk to kill. Who's Momma sent you after?" Tommy asked, matching his volume.

"His name's Marcus Thompson. Momma said you might be able to point me his way." William replied.

"I certainly can. He's playin' stud at that table by the door, the one with the uncomfortable lookin' girl sat on his knee. He's a real shit heel too, big figure in the local knights. Still though, Momma's a pragmatic woman with a lot of heat on her. He must've done somethin' pretty bad for her to resort to this," Tommy said.

William looked at him disdainfully and said to Tommy, "Well if you believe Momma, he almost beat one of her girls to death."

"Which one?" Tommy replied frantically.

"Lucy, I think," William replied. "Why?"

Tommy ignored his question and said, "Damn shame. Lucy's a sweet girl. Wouldn't say boo to a ghost. She OK?"

"I think," William replied, deciding not to press Tommy further on why he cared so much. "I'm not too sure to be honest, kid."

Marcus Thompson sat hunched over a dwindling stack of chips, and with each subsequent loss, the prostitute on his lap grew less and less interested in him. Fat spilled over his collar and draped down under his chin. Flesh formed a bulge on the back of his neck, which rippled with every deep wheezing breath. The deep bellows of his painstaking inhales made his cards ripple and could be heard from the bar. His head was almost completely bald, save for some grey stubble that covered its periphery and thinned out towards his prominent bald spot. Beads of sweat slowly traversed down his chubby face, falling like raindrops as he flittered away the last of his money. Even above that soaring piano, William could make out his chair creaking whenever he moved to bet, even sensing the floorboards as they flexed and bent beneath his weight. William couldn't help but think how Lucy felt as he hunched over her and crushed her throat.

Tommy waited until William had finished observing Thompson. "Listen, William, before you go and get yourself killed, I just need to tell you I really appreciate what you did." Tommy said sincerely.

"You need to stop thankin' me, kid. If you spend the rest of life grovelling, then what was the point of me savin' you in the first place?" William said jokingly. When he saw Tommy was being completely sincere, he added, "Look, kid, I'd be dead if it weren't for dumb luck. I don't dwell on it. We just gotta keep on livin'. What's the point of bein' in the land of second chances if you don't make the most of them?"

Tommy replied, "Well if dumb luck had pushed that log, then I'd be in church right now sayin' my thanks to somebody else. But you saved my life; you gave me a second chance when most folk round here don't give me a first chance. You're a brave man, William, and a fine man at that."

"I ain't brave, Tommy, just an opportunist. But I graciously accept your thanks, and I want to thank you fo' givin' me a place to lie low despite the trouble it caused you. Not many folks are stupid enough to do that for two dollars of whiskey," William replied as he smirked.

"Have you thought about what you're gonna do when Momma tells you what she knows?" Tommy asked.

"I'm gonna find the son of a bitch and put him in the dirt!" William said confidently.

"Well, that's all well and good, but if your man lives in Temperance, then there's only a handful of people it could be. And sure, you could catch Cavanaugh on his own, but the rest of those fellas move in packs. They're never unarmed, and they're hardly ever alone. You may well end up having to take on an entire Klan chapter and the sheriff's desk to boot." Tommy explained.

"Then I'd need to think of some way to get the jump on them. I don't know, Tommy. I'll just have to cross that bridge when I come to it," William said, frustrated.

Thompson, by this point, was about six drinks down. He was looking a little antsy as he gambled away the last of his money. He periodically soaked up the sweat stream that ran down his face, using an old sodden handkerchief.

William watched him squirm over the rim of his whisky glass. As it became clear he couldn't pay her, the girl on Thompson's lap got up to leave. He drunkenly grabbed at her wrist and shouted, "Where you goin', honey?"

She swung back and slapped him across the face, shouting, "Take your hands off me, you fat creep!"

He balled up his fists beneath the table, but when he remembered he was in public, he released his grip and grumbled, "You'll be back, sweetie." The stench of whisky poured from his fat lips.

As William watched in disgust, Tommy asked, "What exactly is your plan here? Unless you just gonna watch him to death."

"I didn't even know who he was until you told me. I ain't got a plan yet." William looked at the stack of empty glasses in front of him and continued. "Then again, the man's gonna have to piss at some point, ain't he?"

"That's your plan." Tommy chuckled.

"Yeah," he said cautiously. "Why's that funny? It'll work."

"Oh, I'm sure it'll work. Just don't seen too gentlemanly is all," Tommy said, still smiling. "If you were to pick a fight with him, I'm sure he'd duel you no questions asked. You gotta be faster than that fat fuck."

William scrambled for some reason not to duel him besides cowardice. "I can't draw that much attention to myself," he said. "Anyway, I'd say rottin' in his own shit is about what he deserves."

"Well, when you put it like that," Tommy said. He added, "You ever done this before—what you're about to do?"

"Almost, once. But I have a drive now, a purpose," he said unconfidently.

"Maybe you don't have it in you, Will. Maybe you just ain't got the nerve to kill a man who's never wronged you. There ain't no shame in that" Tommy said.

"Maybe I didn't have it in me. But people gotta adapt sometimes," William said as the life drained from his eyes.

Both the men shuddered as they heard the unmistakable sound of Thompson's chair scraping across the floor. William's eyes homed in on the creeks, followed by the sound of floorboards wailing beneath Thompson's weight. William watched as Thompson began to limp away from the table. He slowly shambled and tried to keep his weight on his good leg wherever possible. Clearly the moving did his wound no good, as it began to seep fresh blood through his bandages and into his tattered trousers.

As the back door swung shut behind Marcus, William downed his drink and strode for the back door. Tommy watched him leave with a terrified expression, not taking his eyes off that door for the entire time they were out there.

William moved fast and silent, finally glimpsing Thompson's white shirt through a crack in the outhouse door. William pulled out his revolver before coming to his senses and tucking it back away. He instead picked up a weighty, rounded stone and waited by the door for it to open. He stared at the ancient wooden plank that stood between him and Thompson, focusing on its rusty hinges and its fraying rope handle in an attempt to stop himself from dwelling on what he was about to do.

There was no lock, but those rusty hinges would no doubt scream if he opened it, and William didn't fancy his odds in a fair fight. He stood to the side of the door, waiting for Thompson to emerge. As the music from the saloon built to a crescendo beneath a chorus of bellowing drunks, Thompson pushed open the outhouse door, doing up his fly as he stumbled out. William brought the stone down on his temple and, as he slumped unconscious, pushed him inside the outhouse.

William stared down at the wheezing body, which lay across the outhouse seat, not knowing quite what to do next. Though Thompson was still breathing, William was frozen in place as he looked down at the dent he'd carved into Thompson's head. His eyes drifted to the blood-soaked stone as he remembered the sensation of cracking the man's skull. William dropped the stone in shock as that crack echoed down his spine.

The times he'd imagined doing this, he'd imagined using a gun, but this was a different thing entirely. Thompson's neck hung over the edge of the bench, and William contemplated just stomping on it. However, this was more brutish than using a rock, and it nearly made him gag. He thought about the lockless outhouse door and the packed saloon of people who may well discover them at any point, and he decided he needed to hide Marcus.

After a few seconds of looking around, William began to heave Thompson off the toilet bench and then ripped up the plank of wood that covered an open cesspit. The thick stench of shit poured from the hole like steam from a kettle spout, but William was far more repulsed by the blood on his hand than he was by the smell. The hole was about four feet deep and only half full, and William slowly began to lift Thompson into it, dodging the splashes of faeces dispersed by his body.

William sat him upright in the filth with his legs either side of the hole. He then placed the board back over the top and stomped until the nails back in place. He panted with exhaustion over the hole, checking to see if Thompson was visible and if he'd gotten anything on him. He stripped off his jacket and used it to wipe his hand as best he could, stuffing it down the hole with Thompson. He picked the bloody rock up and quickly threw it down as well, before peeking out the crack in the door.

When he saw the coast was clear, he sprinted from the outhouse and walked through the saloon's back door. Tommy was incredibly relieved when William walked in but was less happy when he saw the traumatised look on his face. William walked past Tommy and, not wanting to explain what had happened, simply said, "It's done. I'm going to see Momma."

Tommy was concerned for his friend and couldn't figure out how he'd lost his jacket but was happy to see him alive.

William quickly crossed the street and walked up the bordello steps, too shocked to move as cautiously as he should've. William silently paced through the bordello and barged into Momma's office, sweaty and panting. He saw Momma talking to the woman from behind the bar, and he ignored her when she asked him to wait outside.

In a panicked tone, gesturing to Tilly, he asked Momma, "Can you trust her?"

When Momma nodded, William said, "I couldn't kill Thompson. He's in the outhouse outside the saloon."

"He's incapacitated?" Momma asked.

"Yeah, he's unconscious and hidden under the bench," William explained. "I'm real sorry I couldn't do it, Momma," he grovelled.

"You know what, son? I think that'll be more than sufficient" she said as she gestured to Tilly. "You have business to attend to, Miss Tilly. We'll speak after."

Tilly nodded and left the room, closing the door behind her.

Momma continued, "It ain't your fault, son. There's no shame in not takin' a life. You've done most of the work anyway," she said ominously.

As she spoke, William noticed Tilly crossing the street through the big window in Momma's office. William ignored this and asked, "So you'll still help me?"

"I will," Momma said. "All I ask is that you don't run off on a manhunt and get yourself killed immediately."

William replied, "That almost sounds like compassion, Momma."

She replied in a frank tone, "Not quite. The situation's just a lot more complicated than trappin' a fella in an outhouse, and I want you take some time to think about how you're gonna do it first."

"OK, whatever you say," William replied, desperate to know the truth.

"Good," Momma said. "The man who rented that key is Edward Fortner, a founding member of the local wing of the Klan. He hardly leaves his home out of fear he'll be beset upon by the sodomites and heathens who fuel this town's economy. On the few occasions he does go outside, he's usually at a rally or a ridin' party. He's real close with Cavanaugh and the sheriff, though I doubt the latter would care to admit that fact."

"So he's hard to get to is what you're saying?" William asked.

"Essentially. He's rarely alone and even more rarely unarmed. And I doubt you'll catch him outside his home anytime soon. Now considerin' you helped me, I could have the girls put on a little distraction to draw him out. But I ain't willin' to get them killed or nothin'," she explained.

William stuttered. "Maybe I could …" But he couldn't think of anything.

Momma said, "Why don't you take a room for the night and come to me with a plan tomorrow. If that plan involves me or my girls, then I'd be happy to help. If not, then I'm just as content sittin' back and watchin' that asshole die. I'd recommend some sort of distraction; the nature of that distraction is up to you. But its more than likely you'll end up takin' on all those boys at once." As she spoke, she slid a key across the table to William.

"Thank you," William said as he picked up the keys. As he turned to leave, he asked "Is there a bath?"

Momma replied sympathetically, "I'll have one drawn. Get yourself a drink, son. Would you like a girl sent up after you?"

William shook his head and turned to leave.

Momma said after him, "Could you send in Miss Mary please? She's the redhead behind the bar."

William nodded and opened the door. He asked Mary to go in and see Momma before sinking into a bar stool and ordering a drink from one of her co-workers. William twiddled with his keys, thinking to himself.

He'd spend much of the night thinking, at one level of consciousness or another, about what exactly he was going to do—attempting to craft a plan that would somehow get him out of this town alive. Though this was the land of second chances, he'd get no second attempt at what he was about to do; it would be death, or it would be freedom.

CHAPTER 9

No Good Deed!

William awoke from a night of thinking. The little sleep he was able to carve out was haunted by the nightmares of Thompson's skull collapsing. In one dream, he'd look down at his blood-red hands and watch as the liquid climbed up his forearms and ran down his chest; when he'd looked up from his hands, he'd seen nothing but a lonely noose dangling before him. He hadn't slept more than two solid hours the whole night and spent the rest of that long evening mapping out his plan on the ceiling of his room.

By the early hours of the morning, William had come up with a plan just audacious enough to get him out of this alive. William got up, unable to lie immobile in that bed any longer. He still had a few hours of skulking around and thinking before Momma got up, and he used this time to iron out the wrinkles in his somewhat ill-conceived plan. He thought about how he was going to spin it to Momma.

William strode into her office to find her and Tommy sharing a cup of coffee and chatting. William sat in the seat in front of her and again waited until she'd finished what she was doing.

Tommy smirked at William. "Well if it ain't the outhouse outlaw."

"Good one. You take all night to think of that?"

Momma interjected, "Damn near all night. Don't you have a home to get to, son?" She turned to Tommy, who glanced away evasively. "I think you need to give us a little time, Tommy. Me and Mr Lee have some things to discuss."

"Alright, I'll take a walk," Tommy said as he left the room.

"So," Momma asked, "what do you have for me?"

"I think I can get him out in the open, but I'm going to need a little more help from you than you might be comfortable with." Momma didn't look as displeased at this as William was expecting, and he continued. "However, I assure you that you and your girls will be well compensated."

"The penniless fugitive is offering generous compensation," she said sarcastically. "I'm all ears."

"First, are you sure that Fortner would show up if the sheriff pulled together a posse?"

"He'd be there with bells on. Those boys never miss the chance to shoot somethin'." Momma answered.

"Well, in that case, I'm suggestin' we get all our bad eggs in one basket. Then we destroy the basket." William said.

Momma smiled and said, "You have my attention, son."

"I'll set up camp out of town for a few days. Then once we're ready to move, you tip 'em off to my location. I can work around the cliff line and come in through the other side of town while they march off in the other direction. You and the girls set up an ambush in the streets while I rob the bank. I should be able to clear the vault and make it to you in time to spring the trap on the sheriff and his ridin' party," William explained confidently.

Momma looked baffled and proud all at the same time. "Ambitious," she remarked. "I like ambitious! But you're bettin' that a bunch of prostitutes can ambush a heavily armed posse of ex-Confederate nutjobs."

"I am. But I know first-hand that they're horses are as stupid as they are, which means, if we can make enough noise, then most of 'em will be on the ground before the shootin' even starts. Now, I'll be outta town, so I'll leave the specifics of the ambush to you. But I'd say we've defiantly got the upper hand, especially considerin' all eyes will be on the bank," William explained, stopping hesitantly to see if Momma had any issues with what he'd said so far.

Momma said, "It's a good plan, son. But you're puttin' a lot of risk onto some innocent women who may've never even shot a gun before."

William replied, "That's why you'll take the cash. I won't need more than a few hundred dollars to make it to Mexico and start afresh, so the rest'll go to you and any of your girls dumb enough to stand with us."

"Hence the compensation you mentioned," Momma said.

"Exactly." William replied.

Momma thought for a moment and said, "Well, we'll need more then side arms, but I'm sure the gunsmith's arm can be twisted, assumin' his wife's within earshot. Will you be needin' anythin' on your end?"

"Some dynamite for the vault and a rifle wouldn't go amiss." William answered.

"There's some dynamite in the cellar. The rifle will be waitin' for you here when you come to join the fight. I'll send word to you if I see anythin' in town you need to know about. You should know, cowboy, we're puttin' a lot of trust in somebody we barley know; so if you don't show up in town or disappear with the money, then there will be no ambush, just a growin' line of folk who'd sure like to string you up!" Momma said, her tone becoming threatening.

William nodded, terrified by this old woman. He left the office and asked one of the girls for directions to the cellar. He climbed down a splintered old hatch behind the bar, which led to a dusty brick basement. One of Momma's girls passed him an oil lantern, and he scanned around the piles of junk in the room, not really knowing what he was looking for.

He eventually found a big red crate. The lid was covered in warnings, and when he heaved it open, an avalanche of dust cascaded off it. William marvelled at its contents; it was half full of bundles of dynamite. He quickly moved the oil lamp out of fear it would somehow ignite the sticks. William pulled out a few sticks from the box and put them in a burlap sack before heading for the shaft of light that marked the cellar exit.

As he climbed out with the sack, he noticed an ominous silence hung over the bordello. Those patrons who had been visiting at such an early time had cleared off. When he went into Momma's office, she ignored him. She stared out the window, and her eyes seemed fixed on Main Street. After not acknowledging William, she suddenly turned and shouted, "They have Tommy! We need to move now!"

William sprinted to the window to see Butch Cavanaugh casually whistling as he dragged Tommy behind his horse. Cavanaugh slowly trotted north, clutching his reins, and yanking on the rope that clamped around his ankles. Tommy fidgeted and grasped at the rope as it wrapped around Cavanaugh's own boots on his feet. As William gawked in shock, Momma unpacked a rifle from a gun case in the office. She clicked bullets into the magazine as she shouted, "We ain't got long, Mr Lee. Now I can't be seen to be involved, but they can't exactly hang you twice. You get in position near them, and I'll get on a roof with this thing. When you hear shootin', you need to get to Tommy and get the hell out! I ain't gonna kill him, but you should be able to steal his horse before he catches his bearings. Get to safety, and I'll tip the law off tomorrow. Make sure you don't get the kid killed. And whatever you do, don't bring him back to town!"

William just nodded and rushed out of her office. Momma shouted after him, "Leave through the back!"

William ran out the back of the bordello and silently shadowed Cavanaugh as he moved down Main Street. He worked down a backroad, watching the two as he took cover beside alleys. He watched Sheriff McKinley run in front of the horse, flailing his arms in the air and screaming, "You can't do this, Butch. It's unlawful, goddamn it!"

Butch, looking furious, said, "Don't preach to me about what's lawful. I'm sick of enabling this little rat. Now those are my boots on his fuckin' feet, so either he helped rob me, or he knows the son'bitch who did!"

"Then why don't you hear the boy out. Maybe he can point you to that fugitive you been after. Let the law get to the bottom of this, Butch. This ain't the way we do things!"

"No more hearings! No more chances! This n*gga has until we reach the gallows to tell me what he knows, or he hangs! This is the law, Sheriff," Cavanaugh said with disgust in his voice.

"There's a process here, Butch. This ain't the way to keep the peace." the sheriff pleaded.

"I'm keepin' the peace, Sheriff, with or without the fuckin' badge. I'm findin' William Lee by sundown, even if I gotta do it without your help!" Cavanaugh said.

He flicked the reins, and his horse began trotting once more. The sheriff stepped aside and let Cavanaugh through. As Cavanaugh passed, he said to the sheriff, "You made the right choice, Sheriff. N*gger-lovers don't win elections in this town!"

The sheriff stared down in shame as Cavanaugh slowly passed by him.

He pretended to ignore Tommy's desperate screams as he was dragged towards the gallows.

From the other side of town, an enormous bang echoed. The volume of the noise almost smashed windows, and it terrified the groups of curious townsfolk who'd been watching the commotion. The sheriff jumped back, startled, and dashed for cover from the gunshots. Cavanaugh was, once again, thrown from his horse, the skittish and untamed nag bucking as the bullet bit the ground around its hooves. Cavanaugh flailed in the air as he hurtled back and tumbled into the earth.

William, finally able to more than just watch, charged out of the alley. He booted Cavanaugh in the face as he was reeled from the fall. William then ran over to Tommy and desperately clawed at his leg restraints. Momma fired another shot whenever the sheriff attempted to move from his cover or when Cavanaugh got too comfortable. William finally undid the rope and helped Tommy to his feet.

Tommy said, "You're sure makin' a habit of this, ain't you, cowboy!"

William replied, "Don't thank me, kid. You got friends in high places."

The two men bolted to Cavanaugh's horse. The beast was anxious at first but calmed down as the gunshots halted and Tommy petted its mane. Both men climbed atop the horse, and kicked dust south.

Cavanaugh groaned for a few moments and clutched his battered head, but when he realised William Lee was once again leaving atop his horse, he clambered to his feet and reached for his pistol. By the time he'd stood up, the men were already out of range, so he cautiously lowered his gun, his hands trembling with fear. Momma calmly and steadily rose her rifle's sights up to his bloated chest and contemplated just killing him right there. But she thought better of it and slowly lowered her gun. After all, Butch Cavanaugh's time would come.

Cavanaugh was dumbstruck, and as he watched the men ride away, he began to gaze around, paranoid, at every roof and water tower in Temperance. He scanned every building or balcony for the silhouette of a person or a rifle. However, the haze and the heat kept Momma's position obscured. Cavanaugh soon gave up on staring at rooftops as his vision blurred. His reopened head wound began to bleed, though not as much as it had before. Cavanaugh limped north up Main Street, seething silently as he held the gash on his scalp.

As the dust settled, the sheriff crawled from his hiding place, and people began to go about their business as usual. The sheriff got onto a balcony and proudly proclaimed that it was safe to go out and that law and order would be maintained in "my" town.

The people of Temperance, who knew little of law and order, ignored him and continued with their lives. A few gathered around the sheriff as he gave a long-winded speech about liberty and community. But this speech was cut short as people began to laugh at him, and he shamefully scuttled off back to his office. McKinley's brave and tireless work had restored order to Temperance. The crowd dispersed, the blood dried, and normalcy returned; however, Temperance was a powder keg, and torches gathered in the north.

CHAPTER 10

Mousetrap

Momma sat patiently with her back against the short wall, which ran around the edge of the bordello roof. She slowly disassembled her rifle as the hustle and bustle returned to the streets. Packing up the pieces into a sack and leaving it on the roof, Momma slowly crawled over to the hatch into the bordello and climbed down. Tilly waited at the bottom of the stairs for Momma and walked behind her. As Momma stretched and rolled her shooting shoulder, she said, "Tilly, dear, would you mind fetching that sack of parts from the roof at some point?"

"Sure, Momma." Tilly said tensely.

"Now don't bring it down until later. I'm sure we'll get an impromptu visit from the sheriff at some point soon." Momma said.

Momma began to pace down the stairs to her office, but Tilly shouted after her. "Um … Momma." She lowered her voice as she glanced around to see if anyone was within earshot.

Momma turned around impatiently before seeing Tilly's face.

She said in a hushed tone, "Is Tommy all right, Momma?"

Momma smiled at her and came a little closer before saying, "Better than all right, Kids got a new horse. Don't worry, Tilly. It don't matter how stupid that boy can be, id never let anything happen to him."

Tilly sighed with relief before looking embarrassed and trying to change the subject. "So, the outlaw did good then?"

"I guess he did, almost good enough to give me confidence." Momma said.

"Confidence in what?" Tilly asked.

Momma turned to continue walking and said, "He wants to rob the bank to drive Fortner out of hidin', and I agreed to help."

"Fortner. The bank. What the hell are you talkin' about, Momma?" Tilly said, confused.

"It's one of those high-risk, high-reward situations. It could get us far away from this town. But," Momma said, "it won't be easy. I'll explain later."

As Momma reached the bottom of the staircase, she heard a violent banging at the door. Suddenly, a deep and familiar voice called out, "Clear out, fellas! I don't wanna find out a thing ya'll don't want me to. I've got business with the owners."

Momma recognised the sheriff's voice, and clearly her few patrons did as well, as they scattered out the back door and went home to their wives. Momma straightened up her hair and her cufflinks and nodded for one of the girls to let him in.

The sheriff waltzed in the door, his obnoxious spurs whizzing as he walked. A gust of cool wind wafted in with him as he strolled in. He immediately locked in on Momma, who watched imperiously from the bottom of the stairs. "Ain't you lot a sight for sore eyes," the sheriff said in a sarcastic tone.

Most of the girls smiled politely, accustomed to hiding disgust around despicable men. However, Momma was not and instead glared at him with distain.

The sheriff grinned at Momma and asked, "Should we go into your office?"

"I'm sorry, Sheriff. I ain't for sale. We got plenty of other girls though." Momma joked.

"I didn't come here to mingle with harlots. I'm here for answers, so you can tell me here, or you can tell me in your office!" the sheriff asserted.

"I trust my girls, Sheriff. So, you best ask what you came here to ask!" Momma replied in a fiery tone.

"Calm down now. I can assure you I wouldn't disrupt these ladies makin' an honest livin' without due cause," he said condescendingly. "As you no doubt know, Momma, we just had a bit of a commotion on Main Street. Did you happen to see any of that?"

"Well, I certainly heard a commotion, but I was too scared to do more than watch." she said innocently, but the sheriff saw right through this.

"We've known each other a long time, Momma. So I know you ain't as meek as you like to make out." He paced closer to her and raised his volume slightly. "Fugitives are robbin' bounty hunters while unknown accomplices take shots at lawmen, so you'll appreciate my frustration as you choose to play games and obstruct the good work of justice!"

Momma looked straight at the furious man and said confidently, "Speakin' of the good work of justice, Sheriff, why is it left up to fugitives and their accomplices to stop an innocent man bein' hung in your town?"

Momma and a few of the girls smirked.

After a few moments of speechlessness, he finally stuttered, "Well … that ain't … All right, this ends now, you goddamn gorgon. You're comin' across town for further questionin'!" he screamed.

"I can follow you shortly if you'd like. But I have some business to deal with here first." Momma said calmly.

"You can walk with me now, or you can answer my questions from the comfort of a cell!" the sheriff snapped.

Momma waited for a few moments while the sheriff's pulse lowered before saying, "How long till Election Day, Sheriff?" The sheriff looked perplexed by this, and before he could answer, she said, "Ten days by my count. Now how does it look when you're seen draggin' an old woman to prison for the alleged crime of preventing a murder?"

The sheriff replied, "I think it looks like order, providin' people are made aware that you assisted in the escape of criminals."

"That ain't the issue, Sheriff—because if you arrest me, then my trial will come before that election. Then you can explain, in front of the jury and under oath, how you let Cavanaugh almost lynch a man in broad daylight while you stood and watched. The day of my trial would be your last day as a public servant in this county, so you best think about that before you level any more threats at me." Momma explained in a stern and calculating tone.

The sheriff went to reply with something bold and stupid.

However, Momma interrupted. "Just leave it, son. I think you've suffered enough humiliation today. Why don't you just go to your office, and I'll follow you shortly." she said, coldly.

The sheriff went to speak. However, he stopped when he saw Momma's piercing and terrifying gaze. He simply turned around and left the bordello, his tail between his legs.

Once the sheriff had gone, Tilly was finally able to go up to the roof and retrieve the sack. Momma ordered all the doors locked to stop the horny drunks filtering back in, and she quickly went to the toilet to scrub the scent of fresh gunpowder from her fingers.

As Tilly was placing the weapon in her office, Momma entered behind her and shut the door. Momma began to speak. "Theres some things we need to get in order before we go ahead with this, the outlaws gonna need all the help he can get." she said before Tilly even realised she was there.

"How exactly we gonna help him?" Tilly asked.

"He'll rob the bank while we set up a little trap for the boys who've been chasin' him," Momma calmly explained.

"Half the goddamn town's been chasin' him!" Tilly shouted.

"Keep your voice down, Tilly. I haven't told the others yet. I'll explain it to 'em, and those who can't or won't fight won't have to. Those that do chose to fight will have the high ground and the element of surprise. I don't think we'll need more than three or four guns on the roof to pull this thing off." Momma said.

"Why, Momma? Why risk everything to save some guy you don't know?" Tilly asked.

"It's not for him, Tilly. It's for you and Tommy and Lucy and all the other people this town is killing. People like us just can't build a life in a place like this, especially when I'm not here to protect you lot. I ain't got long in this world, Tilly, and I don't wanna die knowin' everyone I love will follow suit. I ain't askin' anyone to get killed for this, and I'll make sure nobody's put in harm's way. But for that, I'll need the help of capable people like you. What do you say, Tilly?" Momma implored, placing her hand on Tilly's shoulder.

"I just don't know why you're betting all our lives on a man we barely know, Momma."

"Because I see a way out in him, Tilly. Do you remember why you came to me in the first place?" Momma asked.

"Of course, I do. I was moving out west with my husband to teach on the frontier, and then—"

"And then he met someone else and left you in the middle of nowhere without a pot to piss in." Momma interrupted. "You were only supposed to be with me for a few weeks. But the world put you in a box and told you that was the only place you'll ever know. I can't leave this world in good conscience without getting all of you out of that box."

"There ain't a person in this building you've not gone above and beyond for, Momma. You don't owe us anything." Tilly replied warmly.

"Look, when I started this place, I wasn't the person I am now. I was just somebody hoping to rise above their place in life by exploiting vulnerable people like you. But the more I spoke to people like you and really heard what you had to say, the more my motives began to unravel. I saw people who were strong and caring and ambitious despite the world's constant attempts to beat that out of them. I found a family, Tilly—a family I simply must leave with more than a shitty bordello in a shitty town! Will you help me, help me get you to that frontier school?"

Tilly contemplated for a few seconds. "Alright, Momma. I'm with you whatever you need." she said confidently.

"Thank you." Momma smiled at her—half expecting everyone to abandon her when they heard about her plan—and went over to a drinks cabinet in her office. She began pouring them both a gin. As she handed Tilly the glass, she asked, "First things first. Would it be possible to squeeze some rifles from that gunsmith next door?"

"The one with the piss fetish and the overbearing wife? It's possible," Tilly joked as she smiled at Momma. "I wouldn't be the best girl to do it mind. Mr Mathews would be far more obliging if Jane was the one askin'."

"Then you find Jane, and you put her on it. We don't have much time before things begin to move out of our control. After that, I'll need some thick rope and maybe a few firebombs if needs be—anything you can think of that would blunt a horse charge." Momma explained.

Tilly smiled and said, "I'm sure I can think of a few things. Anythin' else needs doin', Momma?"

"Yes, there is," she replied as she took some make-up and a pocket mirror from her desk and began to touch up her hair and make-up. She continued, "Once we have the guns, I need you to close up for the day and take a few of the girls shootin' somewhere discrete. I don't need marines.

I just need them pointin' the right direction and stayin' in cover where they can."

"Consider it done, Momma. Who exactly you dressin' up for?" Tilly asked.

"Why, it's a disguise, Tilly. For the next twelve hours, I am, for all intents and purposes, an innocent and righteous woman." Momma said jokingly.

"You don't gotta lie to me, Momma. You're hopin' to impress that sheriff, ain't ya," Tilly responded jokingly.

"I prefer my men have external genitals. Till," she said as she straightened up her clothes, "I'm about to walk into a den of wolves with singular knowledge of where the sheep are hidin', and I've found that people in this town are far more willin' to intervene on behalf of a woman if she happens to look like a preacher's wife. The cries of harlots and n*gros fall on deaf ears in Temperance." she said.

"I don't think McKinley's about all that. He ain't so much cruel as he is weak," Tilly argued.

"It's the same result." Momma responded as she picked up her most effeminate handbag. She continued, "Whip these girls into shape, Tilly, and we might just leave this town alive."

Momma strode out her office and out the front of the bordello as Tilly finished her drink. Momma marched down Main Street to the sheriff's office to see his deputy sitting on the porch, dozing in his chair and nursing a bottle of spirit. He was slumped to the side and half asleep as flies circled his head.

Momma peaked through the open door but couldn't see if the sheriff was inside. She shouted to the sleeping deputy, "McKinley in there?"

The deputy snapped awake and looked around him to see where he was. As he rubbed his eyes, he said to Momma, "Do my eyes deceive me or is the queen of the whorehouse dressed in her Sunday best?" He cackled. "I doubt you dressin' fo' church. You takin' clients again, Momma, because I'm first in line."

Momma looked disgusted and simply emphasised her question. "Is the sheriff in?"

"He is. However, he's a bit busy tryna track down the outlaws and those in this town who conspire with 'em. You wouldn't happen to know anythin' about that, would ya, Momma?" the deputy accused.

"No, I would not. I'm a businesswoman, Mr Preston, nothing more," Momma said as she climbed the steps to the sheriff's office.

The deputy thrust his arm in front of the doorway and looked down at her, spewing his rancid breath all over her. "It's Deputy Preston! McKinley and I are the law in this town. You will show us the respect we deserve, as we show you the respect that you deserve. As for your involvement in this morning's events, when we find that outlaw and the n*gger he rides with, we'll torture them until they tell us who was on the other side of that rifle. If that person happens to be you, then I promise that not only will you swing, but all your whores'll swing beside ya!" he said in a wheezy and raspy voice as he leaned in closer.

As Deputy Preston loomed over her, Momma reached one hand into her purse and grabbed something. The deputy heard a hammer click back as Momma pushed a barrel into his ribs through the corner of her purse. The deputy tensed up as Momma leaned in real close and whispered to him, "You should know, Deputy Preston, men who threaten my girls don't last too long in this town. So, you best move your arm, or you'll find out first fuckin' hand that, when I'm on the other side of a rifle, I don't miss!" she snarled as she shoved the barrel deeper into his abdomen.

He slowly retracted his arm. Momma lowered her purse as she stared down the deputy. He slowly sat back down in his chair and cradled his bottle, refusing to look Momma in the eyes. Inside Momma's purse, her thumb clicked the hammer forward once more, and she slowly ungripped the revolver. She cleared her throat and straightened her hair slightly before walking into the sheriff's office.

It was a small brick and wood building with open doors at the back and front. The doors somehow managed to waft in all the of the dry and choking breeze while letting out none of the heat. The air was thick and sweaty, not unlike the men who breathed it. It stunk simultaneously of damp wood and dried shit.

To the right of the door was a small and faded brown desk piled high with fliers and papers. Sheriff McKinley sat hunched behind the papers, most of which appeared to be Vote McKinley posters for his re-election campaign. He poured over them, but Momma quickly noticed he was just shifting sheets around and pretending to be busy. "One moment please," McKinley said as he raised his finger to Momma. "Take a seat. I won't be long."

Momma hid her smirk as she watched him pretend to do his job. She turned around and walked straight past the chair beside McKinley's desk to the bounty board. He glanced up from his pretend business to size up Momma. He was shocked to see her dressed so nicely but quickly looked back down at the blank piece of paper he'd signed five times.

Momma examined the bounty board and saw William among a sea of Temperance's most notorious. The newer poster of William was slightly more accurate. It raised his bounty to eighty dollars and actually alleged he'd committed the crime Cavanaugh had picked him up for. It seemed, in Temperance, the punishment sometimes preceded the crime.

Momma glanced over to the back corner of the sheriff's office, which was a small drab cell with a wooden plank suspended from the wall and a foul bucket tucked in the corner. It was likely either her, Tommy, or William would see the inside of that cell before the week was out; they may even all share it. It was then she decided she would protect her family or die trying. If the outlaw made a mistake and got caught, then that was on him. But McKinley could have her children over her dead body.

The sheriff looked up from his desk and said in a frustrated tone, "Why is it you see the need to terrorise my deputy, Momma?"

"Sheriff, if you cared about your citizens bein' terrorised in any meaningful way, then that man would no longer be your deputy." she said coldly, still refusing to look at him.

The sheriff seethed for a moment before pointing at the bounty board and saying, "Your friend?"

"Whilst I know Tommy and I seriously doubt the claims Cavanaugh made against him, I can't speak to the identity of the man who saved him." Momma said, choosing her words carefully.

"I'm sure Tommy could speak to his identity. And though you may doubt those claims, I'd say I can at least prove a conspiracy between them." the sheriff said confidently.

"How exactly would you do that, McKinley? Some folks don't just sit back and let a lynchin' happen." Momma said.

The sheriff was enraged by this but continued. "Strangers rarely save each other's lives twice in one week." he said as he smirked.

"Twice?" Momma asked, confused.

"I believe Mr Lee saved Tommy from a Klan attack the other day!" McKinley exclaimed, given a burst of confidence by knowing something Momma didn't.

Momma was taken by surprise but responded quickly. "Isn't that your job, Sheriff? Or do the outlaws keep the law nowadays?" she asked sarcastically.

The sheriff stood up and slammed his desk, shouting, "You think this is a joke? The outlaw was spotted coming and going from your place of work and has a provable relationship with your surrogate son. On top of this, the shots that aided in the escape of two fugitives came from the direction of your fuckin' rooftop! This is not the time stubborn obfuscation. You better start tellin' me what you know, or you can spend the next few days shittin' in that there bucket!" The sheriff reached a screaming volume, and townsfolk could hear him shouting down this old woman from the street.

When he'd finished speaking, Momma calmly replied, "Come now, Sheriff. This behaviour is unseemly. You can lower your volume, or I will simply walk out of this office right now." she added confidently as she watched the veins in his forehead bulge.

The sheriff slowly sat back in his seat, and his breathing slowed; his face returned from pink to normal.

"Good," Momma said. She continued, "As you know, Sheriff, all manner of folk darken my doorstep, and it ain't really in my interests to check for open warrants at the door. As for the gunshot you and your charmin' deputy seem to think came from my roof, that ain't compellin' enough for you to be takin' that tone or tryna tell me where I can shit."

"I happen to disagree; it all seems pretty compellin' to me." the sheriff replied in a more docile but equally aggressive manner.

"Really, Sheriff, because a man was almost lynched in front of you today. If you say Tommy and this outlaw are conspirators, then I could equally say you conspired with Cavanaugh to have Tommy murdered without due process." Momma said as she stared down the sheriff.

"That's ridiculous! How dare you!" the sheriff exclaimed.

"No, sir. What's ridiculous is pinnin' false charges on Tommy in order to justify Cavanaugh's actions and excuse your cowardice." she said. Momma looked at McKinley, who desperately tried to hide how scared he was. "I doubt you could see where the shooter was from behind your mother's skirt, and you've got no way to put me on that roof with a gun, so you best think before you start makin' grand accusations of collusion!" she concluded.

McKinley was stunned to silence by Momma's words. He grappled for a moment before saying, "Are you so goddamn arrogant that you thumb your nose at justice, at everythin' that separates us from the savages out on the plains? You stand in direct opposition to the peaceful runnin' of this town." His volume rose once more. "And when we find Mr Lee, I hope he gives me sufficient evidence to hang you beside him."

Momma paused for a moment before saying, "You are not justice, and you would fail to keep any order without a mob at your back. Don't you fuckin' dare preach to me about savages on the plains, because the real savages are the men who keep your peace!" Momma took a breath to compose herself and slowly said, "I can assure you, Sheriff, if I were in the path of Cavanaugh's horse today, then there would be no need for Tommy to become a fugitive in order to find real justice."

Momma glared down at this pathetic man and the stack of papers he hid behind. She scoffed and said, "Good luck with the race, Sheriff."

Momma strolled out of the sheriff's office and heard McKinley throw a stack of those paper on the floor in frustration. Momma ignored his ravings in her wake. But as she was leaving, she was passed by two large figures. One of them she recognised immediately from his horrid breath and the vacant chair outside. The other took her longer to recognise.

While the deputy's silhouette was tubby and short, the other figure was cut from different cloth. He was a towering shadow whose enormous weight was only concealed by his immense height and some generous shirts. His arms swayed like great pendulums as he stormed in, and the force of him passing so quickly was almost enough to blow Momma from her feet. His giant fists swung like wrecking balls around his huge torso. His hands were large enough to crush Momma's head and were almost at the right height. The two men surged past her so quickly she barely had to time to make out their faces. But as they turned, Momma caught a glimpse of a large scar across the right side of the tall man's face. She knew immediately who he was—Edward Fortner, the most dangerous man in a town of outlaws.

Fortner had been hit by a piece of shrapnel during the war, and since then, he'd made every attempt to hide his wound when he was in public. Rumour had it that Fortner didn't use the oil lamps in his home out of fear someone would see his face. It was doubtful he was that extreme, but even today, he wore a large duster coat with a turned-up collar and a large hat that drooped down across the right side of his face. The wound itself was a deep gash criss-crossed by a thousand different stitches that stretched from just in front of his earlobe to his chin. Fortner was a mountain of a man, and every word he said would bellow from his chest as if it were a church bell.

Momma heard an agonising screech from McKinley's antiquated desk and turned to see Fortner leaning over the small wooden object. He stared down the anxious-looking sheriff like a brown bear peering down at a bunny. Fortner's voice echoed, "This won't stand, Waylon!" in a commanding Southern shout.

Momma swiftly crept around the side of the building. She stopped under a window and checked to see if she could hear anything. When she couldn't make out what they were saying, she slunk around and crouched by the open back door. From here, she could clearly hear Fortner yelling. "Cavanaugh's on the warpath. He's over with the boys as we speak, stirrin' them up for a lynchin'."

"Look, Ed," the sheriff replied in a relatively weak and small voice, "I appreciate he's angry. But these things have to go through the proper channels." He raised his volume a bit but still kept his tone polite. "I will not plunge my town into anarchy for the sake of Butch's fuckin' ego!"

As Fortner inhaled sharply, Momma could almost hear McKinley's heart skip a beat. Fortner roared, "Chaos! Are you serious!" He leaned further over the sheriff. "You stood by and watched as the n*gro and his outlaw friend made a mockery of your proper channels! Your constituents will pursue justice, Sheriff, with or without your help!"

"I get that you're frustrated, Ed. But think how it looks if I have to keep the peace at the head of a mob," the sheriff implored.

"I don't care what it looks like, Waylon, so long as the peace is kept, and God-fearin' folk are free to go about their business! Either you can call a posse and do what needs to be done, or this whole thing is gonna be outta your hands." Fortner snapped at the cowering sheriff.

"I will put together a posse, but I need some time to find out who the hell was on that roof. Otherwise, we'll only come out of this with two of the three criminals we're lookin' for. I can't let those gunshots go unanswered on the eve of an election." the sheriff desperately explained.

"The gunman isn't going anywhere. Meanwhile, those outlaws slip further from our grasp the more we wait," Fortner explained, continuing in a more ominous tone. "You know who put you where you are, the people who actually voted for you. The only thing those people are going to remember on Election Day is whether you was ridin' with 'em to bring law back to town or whether you're the idiot who let that n*gger run off with Cavanaugh's horse."

Momma, the Sheriff and all of Main Street could sense the tension in his words; this was the last time Fortner was going to ask nicely. "Fine, Ed. If you can give me a few hours to make this all legal and deputise those that are comin', then we can move out first thing tomorrow. But we need to think about appearances, which means no hoods, no torches, and no fuckin' rope. This is a legal posse, not a lynch mob. If Cavanaugh can hold his temper and follow my lead, he'll see then hanged soon enough."

McKinley waited tensely as Fortner thought about his proposal. He finally replied, "OK, Waylon. Butch is a stubborn old fool, but I'm sure he can hold back for a few hours. They rode off in the direction of the old springs south-west of town. If you don't quit draggin' your heels and do somethin', then we're headin' there without you, appearances be damned!" he said in an authoritative voice.

"Understood. Deputy Preston, would you please escort Edward out."

"Yes, sir." the deputy said as he began walking Fortner out into the street.

The deputy went to turn around and walk back into the sheriff's office. But Fortner said, "Walk with me a moment, would ya, Preston?"

The two continued walking until they were out of earshot of the sheriff, and momma followed through the shadows of a side street. Fortner said, "Look, son, I know you don't really know Cavanaugh. But he ain't really the type to do things by the book, especially if that weasel pins a badge on him." he explained.

"What exactly is you sayin', Ed?"

"I'm sayin' McKinley's an idealist with a real soft spot for that blackie. I doubt he's just gonna sit back and let Cavanaugh do what needs to be done. If it comes down to it, I'm gonna need you to escort Waylon back to town before he tries anything he'll regret." Fortner said coldly.

"I don't know, Ed. Maybe he'll turn a blind eye towards Lee, but the charges against the darkie are tenuous at best. I doubt the sheriff will let him die over them." the deputy cautioned.

"Perhaps," Fortner replied confidently, "but what the sheriff won't allow and what he can actually stop are two vastly different things."

"I can ask him to let it go. I just don't think he will is all. He's old-fashioned, obsessed with honour and all that shit." he said.

"If there's one thing Waylon is besides old-fashioned, it's remarkably flexible when given the proper motivation. When the time comes, we will give him that motivation!"

And with that, the two men parted ways. The deputy returned to this chair to sleep until the riding party was ready to move out. Edward Fortner went to find Cavanaugh to tell him what was happening.

Momma disappeared into a winding backstreet of and came out an alley opposite the bordello. She entered to see Tilly handing out repeater rifles to the girls. "Excellent work, Till!" she exclaimed. "We may well be in with a fightin' chance after all."

"A chance at what?" one of the girls asked.

"At survivin' this godforsaken place." Momma replied.

As the girls murmured among themselves, Momma pulled Tilly aside and said to her, "Look, I know you've done enough. But I still need your help."

"You don't even gotta ask, Momma," Tilly said without a moment's hesitation.

"I need you to run a letter outta town to Tommy and William for me. I think they're somewhere near the old spring, but their tracks will probably still be fresh." Momma said.

"OK. You want it done now?" Tilly asked.

"Not yet," Momma replied. "I'll let you know when I've written it."

After she said this, Momma got up onto a chair and began to address the crowd of huddled courtesans. "Now I know ya'll must be confused, but before I explain I need to say that anyone who wants no part in what were doin' will be free to sit out of all this." She paused for a moment and said, "All right then. Now you girls know better than anyone what brutes the men who run this town can be. You're all observant enough to have noticed Mr Lee comin' and goin' from my office recently. So, I'm gonna tell you straight, Lee's plannin' to rob the bank, and he's asked for our help. While he's robbin' the bank, we'll be preppin' an ambush for the legal party on his tail. I know it's a big ask, and they'll be plenty of ways to help even if you don't want to hold a gun, but if we can do this successfully, then we'll make enough money to move far away from this wretched place and start a new life." Momma explained to a room in stunned silence.

The girls glanced around at one another like Momma had lost her mind. Lucy's voice faintly echoed from the back of the crowd. "But why, Momma? Why risk all that?"

"Because there's enough money in that vault for a fresh start, and we can all be investors in that new life. I'm an old woman, and I ain't gonna be here forever to protect you. If I could get you to a better place among better folk, then I could die happy, even if that means it's just me and the outlaw fightin' tomorrow."

Another voice echoed out. "We ain't fighters, Momma."

Momma exclaimed, "Bullshit! You've been fightin' every damn day of your lives, and there ain't a man alive who could hold a candle to one of you ladies. You're among the bravest, the kindest, and the strongest people I've ever met. You're warriors, all you have to do is learn to shoot," Momma implored. "I can't promise we'll win tomorrow, but you ladies should be aware—live or die tomorrow, I'm right beside you!"

A few faces in the huddle began to nod, and a slight murmur fell over the room. Momma said after a few seconds, "All right. Don't keep me in suspense, ladies. Who's with me?"

One by one, a dozen hands rose into the air. Momma smiled sweetly and continued, "That's more like it. How many of you have ever shot a gun before?"

A few of the hands fell, but most remained up.

"Not bad. So how many of you have ever killed anyone before?"

Half the hands fell.

"Well, those who haven't don't need to start now. But we'll need to make a lot of noise if we want to make this work. So, if you don't want to shoot someone, miss on purpose."

Momma climbed off the chair and walked over to Miss Tilly. "Set these girls up with some targets and find out which of them can actually hit somethin'. Once you're done with that, I need you to come back here and collect that letter."

Momma walked into her office and began drafting her letter. She poured over blank pages and was, for the first time in decades, filled with a sense of optimism for the future. If she played her cards right, then she'd be leaving Temperance with a cohort of wealthy prostitutes behind her. However, she wasn't the only one gambling, and Cavanaugh was yet to play his hand yet.

CHAPTER 11

Out of the Frying Pan

As William rode hard away from Temperance, Tommy sat side-saddle. He smiled, as the place which should've been his grave shrunk into the desert. Even as the town became little more than a silhouette on the horizon, Tommy never took his eyes away from it.

Early morning moved to midday, and the sun peaked over those great red cliffs, bathing the valley in its warm glow. Tommy watched the birds above him as they danced in perfect unison. He tracked the swirling dust particles illuminated by beams of light, and he felt every movement of the horse beneath him as it bounced across the sands. Tommy was engrossed by all this beauty around him, a beauty once shrouded the hate and filth of Temperance. It took the horse stopping abruptly to break him from this trance.

"This should be far enough," William said as he slowed the horse and began to dismount, "for me at least."

"Why we're barely outta sight, cowboy. There's no such thing as far enough with the folks we're runnin' from." Tommy said in worried voice.

"And you best get goin'. But I ain't done with this cesspit yet. I need to stay close enough to walk back. But if I was you, I'd ride in circles till this has all blown over. Then I'd get some seed money, and I'd kick dirt 'till I hit the Pacific." William said.

"What for, cowboy? Between us, we ain't had the best luck in that place. What the hell you even got there?" Tommy asked. "I lived there twenty years, and I'm more than ready to cut and run."

"Well, my luck's about to change. I can't leave without doin' what I came here for." William explained as his eyes glazed over.

"Bullshit, you can't! Are you really about to die for your pride?" He paused for a moment. "Death just spit us out. You really wanna get back in his mouth?" Tommy said.

"For enough money," William said with a smirk, "and my pride of course."

Tommy looked confused and said, "What exactly are you plannin' to do when you head back to town?"

"While the sheriff's ridin' around the desert lookin' for us tomorrow, I'm gonna come into town from the north. I'll rob the bank while Momma preps an ambush in town. I should be able to blow open the vault by the time that posse comes back to town and help Momma with the ambush. If things work out, I'll take enough money to go to Mexico, and Momma and her girls can take the rest." William explained confidently.

"You a bank robber, cowboy?" Tommy asked.

"I'm a tanner." William said.

"Really? You do a lotta controlled demolitions as a tanner?" Tommy asked sarcastically.

"I get your point," William said, annoyed.

"Last time I checked, them girls are prostitutes—not soldiers. In fact, I'm pretty sure the only one of ya'll who could pull off a thing like this is a sixty-five-year-old woman," Tommy joked.

"Well then I guess its lucky she's leadin' the ambush." William frustratedly said.

"Maybe I'm bein' a little hard on your plan. I trust Momma to throw one hell of a party for those boys when they come back to town. I just don't trust you to not blow your damn hands off tryna get the vault open." Tommy chuckled.

William scoffed and said, "I'll be fine. It don't seem too complicated."

Tommy began to laugh more. "That's just what folk say before they blow their fingers off."

"Really! How many folks you seen blow their fingers off then?" William said defensively.

"More than I can remember, cowboy, and they all sounded like you do now. Hell, that's how I sounded right before I almost blew my hand off. I used to be a shot-firer. Shit like that happened all the time." Tommy explained.

"Well why don't you just fuckin' show me then!" William snapped.

"Calm down. I'd be happy to. I'd just hate for you to show up to a gunfight with no arms," Tommy said as his laughter stopped. "So, what am I meant to do then, if you're goin' back there?" he asked.

"Well, the way I see it, you have three options—you can either use the bank job as cover to put as much distance between you and this town as possible, you can wait near town for the carnage to be over and then travel outta here with Momma, or you can pull of a bank job with a fingerless tanner and slip once more out of the jaws of death. It's entirely up to you, kid. I'd be just as happy watchin' you ride away to better things as I'd be fightin' by your side." William said.

Tommy sat down on a rock in silence for a while as he weighed up his options. "Well, I can't just leave you empty-handed here, but I ain't no gunslinger." He paused to think things through. "I'll stay with you at least until you go back to town."

William began setting up their camp, and Tommy followed suit, placing rocks in a circle to mark a firepit.

Tommy asked, "Did you find out who killed you wife?"

"Some guy called Edward Fortner. I don't know what he looks like, but I'm sure Momma can pick him out when the shootin' starts," William explained, but as he looked up at Tommy, he saw him frozen with fear.

"Di-did you say Fortner?" Tommy stuttered.

"Yeah. Are you OK, kid?"

"That's, uh … I just hope you succeed," Tommy said, his tone sad.

William asked, "What's wrong?"

Tommy's eyes pointed shamefully down at his feet, as he refused to look at William. He felt himself choke up. He finally managed to say, "He … uh … he was in the posse that killed my pa."

"Jesus, I'm so sorry, kid. That's horrible!" William consoled.

"Why are you apologisin'? You're the feller who's gonna kill him." Tommy said as he suppressed his quivering lip.

"How old were you?"

"Seven. I still remember the sight of him dancin' in the distance as those Klansmen rode away."

William placed his hand on Tommy's shoulder. "And he's walkin' free now?"

Tommy stood frozen in a moment of anguished silence until a single word fell from his lips in a torrent of pain. "Acquitted."

Tommy began to sob, and William could do little more then watch as he fell to the floor with tears streaming down his face.

William was unable to deal with this at first, but he soon went over to Cavanaugh's horse and rooted around for a jug of water. He sat down beside Tommy and offered him a sip. Tommy accepted, wanting anything to dull his burning headache.

William sensed he was woefully unequipped to deal with this situation, so he patted Tommy on the knee and said, "Take as much time as you need." And with that, he continued to unpack the camp and let Tommy have some privacy.

William unpacked bedrolls from the horse and slowly began to bunch up some dried ferns in the centre of his rock circle. Once his nose had cleared and after two minutes of staring at his thumbs, Tommy walked over to William. "You sure that's a good idea, cowboy? It's flat ground around here. The sheriff will see that from miles away." Tommy said.

"That's the point. We're gonna leave here as soon as Momma gives the signal that they're comin'. But if we light this as we're leavin' and we're careful with our tracks, then this should buy us some time." William said confidently.

"If the tanner and his harem can pull off a bank job." Tommy said as he grinned through red and puffy eyes.

William smiled with him. "So, what's the deal with this sheriff? I can't quite get a read on the guy." William asked.

Tommy joined him in crinkling up dry foliage for the fire and replied, "Depends on what you mean."

"I mean is he one of them?" William wondered. "'Because I could've sworn he was before that whole business in town."

"He was—at one point. He used to be an idealistic Dixie boy with more hate than sense. Sure gave my daddy a hard time a things. He was never quite comfortable with what they did to him though. He was never enthusiastic about arrestin' Fortner, but I think it broke somethin' in him when he walked free." Tommy said in an almost sympathetic tone.

"What changed?" William asked as he grappled to understand this man.

"Well, he's always been one for grand speeches. But it was like he stopped believing in what he was sayin'. Momma used to tell me McKinley was soft on me, said I reminded him of all he'd done wrong. After they killed my pa, he started drinkin' and whorin' and gamblin' for a time. In fact, Momma used to tell me the only reason he still wore that star was to stop the next brute pickin' it up after he was gone." Tommy explained.

"You really believe all that?" William said, surprised by this whole new view of McKinley.

Tommy thought for a moment. "I think I do. Mommas usually right about things like this."

"How exactly does Cavanaugh fit into all this? Is he one of them?"

"Not really. It's complicated. I don't think he's ever believed in all the stuff they preach about; I don't think he believes in much of anything. Butch just wants a world a world where he's above the law, and he'll support whoever he's gotta to keep it that way. Some men are hateful. Some men just don't care as long as they're top of the food chain."

"I can't tell if that makes him better or worse or worse than the rest of them."

"It makes him exactly the fucking same." Tommy said disdainfully.

"I guess it does," William said. "How exactly did you and Momma meet anyhow? Because I swear she was going to shoot me before I mentioned your name." he asked.

"It's a long story," Tommy deflected.

"Look around, kid. We have time." William pressed. "How am I supposed to trust you with my freedom if you're hidin' things from me?"

"Well, my mother used to work for Momma. She died in childbirth. So when they got my pa, Momma stepped up. I grew up in the bordello with the girls." Tommy said in a guarded tone.

"She didn't seem like the sentimental type to me." William said.

"Well, you don't seem the bank robbin' type, but folk ain't always what they appear." Tommy replied.

"Did you say she worked with your mother?" William asked as he thought once more about what Tommy said.

"I did. And if you like your teeth where they are, you'll say no more about it!" he snapped.

William was shocked for a moment as he realised what Tommy meant. However, he quickly said, "It's OK, kid. Ain't nothin' to be ashamed of. People do what they gotta to survive. Besides, I'm sure they didn't make it easy fo her to do nothin' else."

"No," Tommy said, still embarrassed. "I'm sure they didn't."

"We don't get to choose who brings us into this world," William said. "My daddy was an alcoholic, and my momma was a matchmaker. We're born where were born, and that's that."

"You ever hate your father for what he did?" Tommy asked.

"No, not so much anymore," William said sombrely. "I think I understand the man he was a bit more now; he was a liar and a brute who took what he wanted and gave nothin' back. He took my mother's children from her because he thought we was his to take. And he died alone—shitting his guts out in a cholera overflow ward. He died knowing he'd made one of his sons hate him forever and he'd turned the other into himself. And I'm not sure which of those would've pissed him off more." William said, and while the look on his face was far from happy, his eyes filed with a cold clarity.

"You built yourself a home and a life. That's something your dad could never appreciate." Tommy said as he attempted to console William.

"No. He wouldn't have. But I still took what I had for granted like he did, and I'll probably spend the rest of my life runnin' away like he did." William said as his heart sunk.

"You've shown more courage these past few days than that sack of shit showed in his whole life. I'm startin' to lose count of how many times you've saved my ass!" Tommy exclaimed.

"I gotta come clean about some stuff, kid." William said as he desperately tried to stop himself from choking up. "I can't help but think I should've died in that valley. Instead, I've dragged all you decent folks into my mess, and it may well get you killed. I'm not a gunslinger. I'm just a coward who got lucky." William confessed.

"So, you ain't a gunslinger. You ain't a bank robber neither. That don't seem like the kinda thing you let stop you."

"And what if I fail?" William exclaimed. "What if I told everyone to put their faith in me just to get them all killed?"

"God saved you, William, nobody else," Tommy said as he looked William in the eyes. "God don't see what we are. He looks past what we may have done. All God sees is what we could be, and you could be just what these people need to make a better life for themselves."

"God don't come into it. I came to this town for revenge, but I couldn't even kill Thompson," William said. "Now I have all these people dependin' on me when I don't even believe in myself."

"It doesn't have to be that way, William. Maybe you didn't come here for revenge. Maybe you came here to help good folk get outta somewhere bad, and you didn't even know it. You don't have to kill Fortner tomorrow. Ain't nobody gonna look down on you if you don't." Tommy explained.

"Well then, what's all this fightin' for?" William shouted.

"It sure as hell wasn't for you. Momma's fightin' for her family. The girls are fightin' for the same. Just because you came here for revenge doesn't mean you have to go through with it." Tommy said.

"Then what would that make me?" William said.

"Better than the next man. Better than your father. Better than Fortner will ever be!" Tommy said as he consoled an exhausted William.

William was strangely comforted by this. Maybe it was the death of his wife that had primed him to think this was all he needed to hear. Maybe he'd been waiting his whole life for someone to tell him that he wasn't his father. William wiped the gathering tears from his eyes and smiled for a moment. He'd never shown these emotions in front of someone before and it made him feel uncomfortable and liberated at the same time.

William embraced Tommy and felt a warmth he hadn't felt since the last time he saw his mother, and Tommy could do little else but smile as this almost stranger hugged him. After a few moments, William awkwardly pushed Tommy away and sat in silence.

William desperately tried to change the subject. "So, what are you gonna do when all this is over?" he said in a frantic attempt to fill the quiet.

"I don't know. I've always hated that town. But I've never imagined being anywhere better."

"Well now you can, where would you go?" William asked as he dabbed dry the last of his tears.

"North—to Canada I guess, or maybe South America." Tommy said as he stared into the blue sky.

"What would you do?" William asked.

Tommy's eyes drifted down to the dirt "I think I'd ... farm something."

"OK. Farming something's a start. Anything in particular you'd like to farm?"

"I don't know. I don't really care. I just think it'd be nice to create something, to make something myself and know it was mine—to know nobody was going to try and take it from me." Tommy said as he picked at a piece of dry grass.

"That's nice," William said as he smiled to Tommy. "I think you've earned that."

"What are you gonna do, Will?"

"I don't really know. I didn't appreciate it at the time, but Abigale was all I had—all I ever needed. I don't think I want a life without her," William said sombrely.

"But you need to go on livin', William."

"I would ... I'd go south-west. I want to see the Pacific."

"The Pacific sounds nice."

"I've always wanted to see the Pacific. Some of my earliest memories are looking out on the docks in Philly. It looked so dark—so grey and empty. But the Ocean off Mexico must be so different, bluer than the sky and bigger than I can even comprehend. I'd find a spot far from civilisation, maybe a spot where no other man had set foot. Then I'd just walk in—try and find Abigale in that vast empty blue, finally tell her I'm sorry." William said as he smiled to himself.

Tommy was unsettled, but that didn't mean he couldn't understand. In William's position, he may well do the same. Both men found themselves looking up. Tommy watched the vultures as they gracefully circled. William looked for Abigale's fingerprints in the sporadic clouds.

Tommy's eyes soon drifted towards the horizon as concern filled his face. He clambered to his feet, keeping his gaze locked on the direction they'd come from. William looked that same way and saw a distant rider followed by a billowing cone of dust. William immediately jumped to his feet and began clutching the six iron in his waist. While Tommy studied the approaching silhouette, William pulled out his gun and began counting the bullets in its cylinder. As he clicked the hammer back, he went to raise the weapon. However, Tommy snatched it out his hands and threw it on the ground, shouting, "What the hell you doin'?"

"We're outlaws, in case you ain't noticed!" William shouted back as he went to pick it back up.

"And don't you look like one!" Tommy shouted as he placed his foot on top of the gun. "Our situation's bad enough without you holdin' up passers-by."

"Excuse me for being cautious." William said in a panicked tone.

"That ain't caution, cowboy. Caution would be stoppin' to think before wavin' a gun around." Tommy said.

The figure became clearer as they spoke, and soon Tommy could see the outline of a dress around the rider's legs. He sighed and said, "At ease, soldier. Unless Cavanaugh's taken up cross-dressing, that's not him."

William finally relaxed and stopped grappling for the gun. He got to his feet and watched in confusion as the figure in the dress approached.

William faintly recognised her face as it came into view. However, he couldn't quite place her, and it only clicked when he heard Tommy say, "Tilly?" as he stumbled towards her.

William examined further back while Tommy ran the distance between him and Tilly. He looked up at her with joy in his eyes. This was a face he wasn't sure he'd see again, and it was the face he'd perhaps miss the most.

Tilly looked down at him and said affectionately, "Hello, stranger. You just can't seem to die?" she joked as she tried to hide the smile that spanned her face.

"You know me, Till. I'm like a bad penny." Tommy replied.

Tilly smiled as she got off the horse and hugged Tommy. "I thought I'd never see you again Tommy." she whispered in his ear as her arms tightened around him.

"We both know you ain't that lucky." Tommy replied.

They broke from the hug awkwardly, and both began walking over to William. He relaxed as he saw Tommy and Tilly hug. As she approached William, Tilly said "You two need to cover your tracks a bit better. I found you and I'm no bounty hunter." She held out some binoculars and a crumpled letter. "Momma told me to give you these. She said you need to keep eyes on the town—sleep in shifts if you have to. William needs to be ready to move fast."

William reached out to take the items from Tilly. However, she kept a hold of them and said, "I hope you know what you're doin', cause Momma's raisin' a militia in town for your ass!"

"This plan'll work," William asserted as he snatched the items from her.

"It better. Ain't just your neck on the line anymore, cowpoke." Tilly said.

She turned from William to Tommy, and her face became warmer. She said to him, "Sorry I can't stay, Tommy. Momma needs all hands on deck for what's comin'."

"It's OK, Tilly. I'll come find you when this is all over," Tommy said.

"You'd better. Don't let this fool get you killed, you hear," Tilly said, pointing at William while not really acknowledging him.

Tommy waved at Tilly as she walked back over to her horse. Tilly must have turned around twenty times in the short walk from the men to her horse. Tommy waved to her, smiling warmly as she mounted up. They looked at one another one final time before Tilly painstakingly turned and rode in the other direction, both tried to hide their sadness as the other disappeared out of sight.

As she left, William said, "I don't think she likes me much."

Tommy replied, still looking a Tilly in the distance, "They're riskin' their lives for you. Do you really need then to like you as well?"

"I suppose not." William said begrudgingly as he opened Momma letter.

Tommy turned and watched William's eyes scan from left to right and said, "Would you mind readin' it out loud?"

"I'll pass it over in a minute," William said dismissively.

"I'd prefer it if you just read it." Tommy said, embarrassed.

William looked at Tommy, who refused to look back. "Sure," he said. "I'll read it out."

He began reading:

> "Things are all good on our end, and the girls are ready
> for a fight. I overheard Fortner and the sheriff talking, and
> they'll be on your tail before nightfall. You'll need to move

fast to avoid them, and if Tilly found you, then you'll need to move a lot smarter. If you boys kept going south, you need to head north-west to a small stream that should cover your tracks. If they don't find you tonight, they'll be back out looking tomorrow. As soon as they leave its all hands on deck. Tell Tommy to wait outside town, and I'll have Tilly pick him up. I swear to God if you bring that kid into a gunfight, I'll shoot you on sight!"

Tommy laughed slightly at this.
William continued:

"Fortner will be in the posse, so make sure you're here on time. There's only so many times my girls are willing to pick up your slack. If your plan works, then you'll have your uncontested freedom and enough money to make the most of it. However, if things go wrong tomorrow, then I will need you to ensure my girls and Tommy get what's theirs and get our alive. After all, Mr Lee, we're criminals with little to lose. They're the people who make any of this worth doing!

Regards,
Momma."

"So, she doesn't want me to help?" Tommy asked rhetorically.

"It certainly looks that way," William answered. "To be honest, I'd feel a whole lot better about this whole thing if I didn't have you with me anyway. It just don't seem right." he added.

"I'm a grown man, Will!" Tommy objected. "I can make my own damn choices."

"Yes, you can. But so can I. And if I make the choice to let you come, then I'm responsible for whatever happens to you." William said.

Tommy attempted to object.

However, William continued. "That ain't even what's important at the moment. We need to move now, or we'll both be swingin'."

"You're right." Tommy said as the two men began to dissolve their little camp.

Tommy folded up their bedroll, while William glanced through Momma's letter again.

The outlaws mounted up and rode north until they came across the small stream not far from Tommy's house. They waded in—though it was only a few feet deep in the centre—and they followed it as it snaked and thinned. They exited the river about a mile down and began to trot up the back of the sheer ridge that hung above Temperance.

As they reached the edge of the precipice, William began unpacking their small camp again, while Tommy walked over to the edge and stood there for a moment. By the time they arrived, it was dusk, and the streets of Temperance were little more than a patch of light veins in the sand. Night fell across the valley and brought with it the biting cold of a desert night.

They could almost hear the music through the still desert air and the stench of fresh sick yet hung in their nostrils. Tommy stood so close to the edge that Cavanaugh's boots half hung over it. He watched as small stones he kicked tumbled down to the ground below. With the unimpeded wind washing over him and the dozen desert birds circling not too far above his head, Tommy felt a new sense of freedom. The faint tickle of the breeze as it washed across his face, the sensation of a breath unhindered—this was something he was willing to fight for.

As he gazed across this tiny town, the only place he'd ever known and the home of all his problems, he thought how unlikely escape had seemed in the past. That place should've been his tombstone, as it was for his mother and father. But Tommy would break the cycle. His cage seemed so brittle and tiny from all the way up here; he could not go back to life within its bars.

Tommy stepped away from the edge and helped William finish setting up. As he laid a bedroll down, he said, "I think I've decided. I'm comin' in with you."

"No way!" William exclaimed, "You know what Momma will do to me if I bring you along. It was stupid you comin' anyway." William argued.

Tommy replied calmly, "I'm a black outlaw in bad country. How far do you think I'll get with no money?"

"Momma wouldn't let that happen. She'll make sure you're taken care of." William said.

"Momma won't get much choice in the matter, because I'll starve in the desert before I'll take a damn cent I didn't earn. Speaking of which, you can have this back." Tommy said as he threw back the money William had left on his table. "It just ain't fair me doing nothing and getting everything."

William sighed. "Fair don't come into it. I'm not takin' you in because it's a Klan shootout, and you're a black man with no shootin' experience."

"No, Will, you look. You've been an outlaw for two goddamn days longer than I have, so don't act like your Billy the Kid. You've never used dynamite, and you've sure as hell never stared down a posse before. So neither of us is really in our comfort zones anymore!" Tommy shouted.

"Calm down," William said in a much more subdued tone. "Have you ever been shootin' before?"

"Well ... no," Tommy stuttered. "But how many of those prostitutes have?"

"Probably quite a few, Tommy. And what do you suppose would happen if you got separated from the group and one of those boys got a hold of you? Because I'll tell you this—they won't make it quick. I refuse to be the one who tells Momma you're swayin' above Main Street because I let you talk me into this." William said in an assertive but reasonable tone.

Tommy initially looked annoyed before a spark of realisation filled his face. "Then I'll just deal with the vault. I mean, you said yourself, it'll be cleared out before the posse even arrives, which means I can be out of town before anything even goes down. You get to keep your fingers and make sure you're there when Fortner comes back." Tommy rationalised.

"I just can't, Tommy. I can't." William said, demonstrating he had little interest in debating.

"Will," he began sincerely, "my whole life I've faced choices that weren't really choices, opportunities that were never meant for me. I struggled against a lot of folks whose only aim in life is to take my agency from me—to make me into a thing and not a man." Tommy sighed deeply before continuing. "But I am a man, and I'm not willing to let them succeed. I'm not even willing to let them fail because of something outside of me. I am going to go into Temperance tomorrow, and I'm doing it for the same reason you are—because it needs to be done; and I need to be the one to do it."

After a few moments of pure awe, William said, "And you think you could rob a bank?"

"About as well as you could. I mean I know how to use the equipment, and I know that bank. I know the vaults, the exit. I know there's a shotgun mounted under the counter. I still might come out with no fingers, but I'll come out in a lot better shape than you would."

"I'd just be worryin' the whole time if I took you back to that place." William said in a compassionate tone.

"You ain't my momma, cowboy. You have enough to worry about without lookin' out for me." Tommy said.

"It ain't like that," William said, "When I came to this place, all I cared about was revenge. But this ain't really about Fortner anymore. I came out of nowhere and blew your fuckin' world up. Maybe I can pay you back for what you've done by getting you to a better place. Maybe that would make it all worth it. I want to help you people wrestle back some of what this town has taken from you over the years," William said passionately. "Then its more than just pride; its somethin' worth dyin' for!"

"Don't I deserve to work for my own freedom?" Tommy replied. "Those girls will have a better chance with you beside them from the start. They've gotta be worth dyin' for too."

William was finally speechless, and after a few moments of tense silence, he frustratedly said, "OK, Tommy. You win. You can come, but you need to promise me that you won't do anything stupid and get yourself killed. When things kick off, you kick dirt. Take the money, get out, and don't come near that place until you're sure it's safe."

"Thank you, William. This'll work!" Tommy assured him.

"But it might not, and if the worst happens, then you and Tilly need to gather up the girls who made it out and leave." William said.

"I can do that," Tommy said.

"Can you? Because if you're sayin' it that confidently, then you clearly haven't grasped what the worst would look like. You need to know for certain that, if me and Momma end up danglin' in the gallows, you'll do the right thing." William said frankly.

Tommy thought in silence for a moment, finally realising the gravity of his situation. "I pray it doesn't come to this, but I think I could do it." he said sombrely.

"That's good enough for me. I won't make you dwell on it anymore. But if you start gettin' foolish notions about revenge when you hear those gunshots, just remember where that got me." William said.

After some contemplative silence, William asked, in an attempt to break the cloud of quiet, "I wonder what Momma's got in store for tomorrow?"

"That woman's been bitin' her tongue and pullin' her punches for twenty years. I think she's gonna burn that place to the ground." Tommy said confidently.

"I'm sure she will. Seems a formidable woman." William said.

"You don't know the half of it," Tommy replied. "Hell, she's the smartest person I've ever met."

"And here's me thinkin' them books were just for show." William responded.

Tommy chuckled, "That sure is one intimidatin' bookcase, and I'm pretty sure she's read 'em all. She spent years tryna teach me, but I could never quite figure out the words. I used to see 'em backwards." he said as he staired off blankly and reminisced to himself.

"Maybe you could have another crack at it. If all goes well tomorrow, then you'll soon be a rich farmer with nothing but time. What do you have to lose?" William asked.

"Well." Tommy racked his brain for some reason to hold him back, but he found nothing. "Nothin'. I suppose I've got nothin' to lose." And as he said this, a small smile graced his face, a fleeting moment of hope in a hopeless few days.

"Everythin' that held you back in that place for your whole life, it don't have to hold you back forever. You'd be a free man in free country, and all you have to do is leave Temperance behind you." William said optimistically.

"I guess so." Tommy said as his mind raced, considering a world with broader horizons then he'd ever experienced before.

William stood up and watched the town in the distance. He marvelled at a small crowd that had formed on main street until he finally realised what they were gawking at. In the centre of the crowd, William could see two distant figures staring one another down. He felt the tension even from here, and it mounted as the two figures squared up. The noise and the chatter from the street drew quieter until, suddenly, both figures snatched at their hips and swung their side irons up. After three seconds came two flashes of light; one man fell to the ground clutching his abdomen. The undertaker had already stripped the dying man of his boots by the time the noise of the gunshots finally reached them.

For an event that seemed so distant, William was intimately horrified by this, and he said to Tommy, "You know I've always wondered, how did a place like that wind up with the name Temperance?"

"Used to be a Quaker town before the war, but the local tribes were real fierce and drove them farther west. This place was abandoned for a time—until somebody found gold in these cliffs. The Indians made sure that the only folk who moved here were those greedy enough and tough enough, mostly outlaws and ex-Confederates. They've long since sucked the last gold from the cliffs, and this place hasn't been the same since." Tommy explained.

"Ex-Confederates and gunslingers, huh. Those fellers paintin' the streets with their stomach linin' sure don't strike me as gunslingers." William remarked.

"Well, the town's changed a lot since the glory days. They're laid-off miners for the most part—drinkin' away their severance pay before their wives catch wind." Tommy said.

"Well," William said, "we've all been there."

Both the men laughed for a second and forgot their troubles.

When he looked back towards Temperance, his troubles came flooding back. He immediately ducked to the floor and began scrabbling around in the dark looking for the binoculars. Tommy went to ask what was happening, but William interrupted. "We got movement!" he hissed in a terrified tone.

Both men sprinted to the cliff's edge and laid down, observing the town. Tommy squinted at the town until Main Street came into focus. He could see, slightly obscured by the light from the saloon, torches gathering. "You think it's our posse?" William asked as he handed Tommy the binoculars.

Tommy didn't answer and simply watched in silence as the cluster of men moved down Main Street. The posse cut through the crowds who'd come to watch the gunfight. Tommy recognised those silhouettes from every visit in the night. He slowly lowered the binoculars in abject horror. "It's a posse all right." he stuttered as the binoculars fell from his hands. "But they're no lawmen."

William snatched them and looked again. He could now see faint hoods and cloaks in on the riders. He slowly uttered, "Jesus Christ, here we go."

Tommy looked mortified, and he began to hyperventilate; his fists clenched shut around some clumps of dirt, and he was visibly distraught.

"Don't worry, kid. They have no bloodhounds and no clear trail. Those geniuses couldn't find their own shadows. They'll find our old camp and then get frustrated and head home." William reasoned, attempting to lower Tommy's pulse.

William understood why Tommy was anxious, and they were both aware that, if they were caught tonight, then they'd never see the inside of a courtroom; they'd be dancing from a tree by morning.

Tommy shivered as he recalled the sensation of that course rope pulling tight around his windpipe. His fingers scanned over the swirling marks indented on his neck by the rope. Tommy stepped back from the cliff's edge and stumbled backwards to the floor; the silhouette of his dead father flashed every time he closed his eyes.

William was concerned for Tommy but stayed on lookout until the riders had disappeared into the distance. As they did so, William said, "Their headin' off in the opposite direction, kid. We should just be thankful we moved camps."

Tommy didn't respond to this, and he recoiled in fear when William went to pat him on the shoulder.

"Maybe we should get some sleep. I can take the first shift." William said.

Tommy took a good few seconds to get out of his own head and formulate a response. "No, it's all right. I'll take the first shift." he said.

"I really don't mind—"

"No, really," Tommy interrupted. "I don't think I can sleep anyway." And as he said this, he retreated into his own thoughts.

"If you like," William said. "Make sure you wake me if we're dyin'. I wouldn't wanna miss the fun." he joked.

Tommy didn't respond and instead walked over to the cliff's edge in silence and picked up the binoculars.

As William settled into the bedroll, he said to Tommy, "Don't drive yourself crazy or nothin'. Wake me if you feel you need to."

But Tommy once again ignored this and took a cigarette from his pocket. His hands shook as he attempted to strike a match. He snapped four of them before he managed to get one lit.

He slowly inhaled and exhaled as he attempted to claw his blood pressure back down. However, he couldn't stave off horrid thoughts and dreadful fears. He looked back up at the birds to calm himself and occasionally threw a stone from the precipice. Tommy could do little but attempt to ignore his dark thoughts; he waited for the reaper or untold riches, whichever found them first.

CHAPTER 12

The Ties That Bound

"William! Wake up! You need to see this," Tommy shouted as he shook William awake.

William, only half conscious, began to rub his eyes open and asked, "What's happening?"

Tommy held out the binoculars and shouted, "Look!"

William snatched the binoculars and shambled to his feet. He walked over to the cliff's edge. However, as the town came into focus, Tommy yanked him to the ground and said, "Stay down! They're close."

William wanted to snap at Tommy. However, he was distracted by what he saw in the valley. His heart leapt into his throat as he watched a pack of torches race in their direction. Now William was awake, and he studied the riders' movements as they bounced across the empty desert. They men froze in desperate apprehension as they hoped for some change in the riders' trajectory.

Not far from the slope that led up to the outlaws, the torches came to a screeching halt and began to form up as the man at the front of the posse addressed the others. William gave a sigh of relief and lowered the binoculars. However, Tommy quickly picked them up as he realised where they were. Although it was near invisible from up here, as all the lights were off and the bleak wooden structure seemed to absorb light, Tommy's house was down there.

Suddenly, the riders fanned out and began to circle the home, illuminating it in a swirl of torches. The outlaws could hear the voices of the Klansmen as they screamed and hollered like banshees. They let off sporadic volleys into the air, and each gunshot was accompanied by a wave of chants and jeers.

One of the riders dismounted and approached Tommy's doors. He rapped three times at the frail wood before stepping back and putting his boot through it. The plank shattered into two large pieces as it flung from its hinges; the Klansman stepped over it and began to search the house. He scoured the small structure with a lantern in one hand and a Litchfield rifle in the other. His fellow spectres paraded around the perimeter, waving their weapons wildly and howling like men possessed.

The dismounted Klansman cleared every room in Tommy's modest shack. As he entered Tommy's bedroom, he fired a shot into the empty bed sheets before patting down the shape in his bed to see if he'd hit anything. The outlaws could see the muzzle flashes through Tommy's window and could do nothing but watch as a few more Klansmen dismounted and began to toss and trash the place.

Tommy stared in stunned silence as the rider emerged from the home and turned to his circling compatriots. "You were right. They weren't stupid enough to come back here." he hollered in a deep Southern twang.

A deep, gravelly voice bellowed out from under another one of the hoods. "It was worth a try. We'll give it another shot tomorrow with McKinley and the dogs. Don't worry, Butch. They can't've got far." he said, turning to one of the other hooded men.

The Klansman, who sounded increasingly like Fortner, tossed a whisky bottle to his friend and said, "You know what to do."

The Klansman laughed as he stuffed a handkerchief into the neck of the bottle, shook it slightly, and took some matches from his breast pocket. "I always hoped we'd do this with him inside." he said as he lit the top of the handkerchief.

"Well, if we catch 'em, we'll burn the place a second time!" He cackled.

To the tune of thunderous applause from the circling riders, he threw the bottle through Tommy's open doorway and began to mount up. The fire raced across the ancient wooden floor. It crawled its way up the walls, devouring the curtains and the sparse furniture. Flames danced across every surface and punched holes in the thin walls. The tinderbox roof soon caught ablaze. Huge pillars of fire poured out every window, crackling and scattering smashed shards across the barren sands. A great plume of smoked raised high into the still air and hung around the outlaws on the ridge.

The riders began to mount up as the cheers from their confederates blended with the roaring of the flames. The men calmly rode off in the direction of Temperance, slowly removing their hoods and stashing them away in their saddlebags.

As limbs of the fire consumed his roof and reached high into the silent night sky, Tommy began to sob, watching all he had being destroyed. William tried to comfort him, but he had no words that could console him, no solace for a thing as heinous as this. Tommy wailed into the quiet abyss, "They've taken everything from me." as the light from the fire glistened across his streaming tears.

William stopped trying to think of some combination of words that would fix this and simply hugged Tommy, who broke down on William's shoulder. William warmly placed his hand on Tommy's head and said, "I know, kid. I know. But we're gonna take it back. I promise."

Tommy fell to the floor in exacerbated agony. He and William just sat and watched the searing flames strike high into the air. The blaze was so tall it looked as if it could scorch the stars, and it burned so bright it almost dwarfed the saloon's glow. This gleaming beacon burned bright against the black tapestry around it, illuminating this decrepit wasteland for miles around.

Tommy cried until he'd finally expended enough energy to take his shift of sleeping. He clambered into the smoke-stained bedrolls and tried to ignore the smell of all he had being put to the torch. Tommy took some much-needed but restless sleep as William stayed on lookout.

The sheriff would ride out to see what the commotion was with his newly unhooded deputy. William chose not to wake Tommy as he knew that McKinley was likely only out here to discover what he'd have to cover up tomorrow. As McKinley sombrely sifted through the ashes, his deputy suggested this was likely an accident and not in the taxpayers' interests. The sheriff ignored this and soon turned to his deputy with a look of disappointment as he found shards of green glass among the embers.

The lawmen rode back to town in unbroken silence as the crumbling remnants of the house smoked behind them. Perhaps he was growing cold in his old age. Or perhaps that star had blackened his heart. But the lawman chalked this up as one more law he would have to ignore, another stain on a greying soul. However, in a rare and intimate moment of self-reflection for men of this calibre, McKinley felt appalled by his immediate impulse to bury this awful act. It seemed that even the sheriff could no longer maintain his delusions under the simmering light of that fire.

CHAPTER 13

Phoenix

William stayed up the rest of the night watching the town, figuring that Tommy could use the rest. After twelve hours of sitting on a rock and chain-smoking the time away, the dawn rose triumphantly behind them and poured into the valley. William was as dead as the ferns around him and as thirsty as the dirt beneath him. But as much as these two sensations pecked at his fragile psyche, the boredom was far worse.

As the sun crested the horizon and bathed his shoulders and back in hot light, he became filled by an artificial energy. Something, undoubtably a combination of adrenaline and sleep deprivation, made him feel good about today. He had entered this valley marked for dead. Yet, while he was almost certainly still a dead man, he may well end up a rich one to boot.

William slowly walked over to Tommy, moving cautiously as to not startle him after the night he'd just had and carefully woke him, saying, "Come on, Tommy. It's time."

Tommy snapped awake so fast that William wasn't sure if he'd even slept.

"What time is it?" he groaned.

"It's morning. We need to move." William replied.

"Did you stay up all night?" Tommy asked as he rubbed his eyes.

"Yeah. So, I don't wanna hear any bullshit about you bein' tired." William said jokingly.

Tommy was in no mood for jokes and simply replied, "Thank you."

William awkwardly changed the subject. "You should get up. I doubt we've got long."

"OK," Tommy said as he began to roll up his uncomfortable bed sheets.

The men packed up their tiny camp and carried it back to their horse, which was tied to a stump about twenty feet from the cliff's edge. As Tommy untied the reins and got the nag ready to move, William went back over to the edge and began to survey the town for any sign of activity. He wouldn't have to wait long.

An ominous silence hung over Main Street that morning, a silence perhaps common in the desert surrounding Temperance but almost unheard of in the town itself. The people still chatted, the drunks still staggered home clutching their heads, yet the streets were unusually quiet. Everything from the rodents to the high rollers observed this eerie silence. They could all feel that something was about to happen. Yet silence was still the only thing that separated this day from another—that is until men began to gather outside the sheriff's office. Every eye in Temperance followed this pack of men as they formed up at the steps to McKinley's office—every eye except for Momma's, which instead squinted at the ridgeline from the porch of her bordello.

Soon enough, those distant specks on the ridgeline began to work their way north. Confident they were on the move, Momma too began to watch the pack of men as they called out for McKinley. There were about a dozen in all, some mounted and some leading their horses in tow—twelve men in enraged and impatient silence, like knights marching sombrely to war. But there was no war, just the wolf pack and its prey.

All of them carried guns, and a few even had the outline of rope in their saddlebags. Cavanaugh emerged from the group and shouted up the sheriff's steps, "Come out already!"

A few of the other men grunted.

"Quit stallin'!"

Finally, the sheriff emerged. He looked pale and deflated from the night's events. His deputy followed behind with a look of boyish excitement on his face. "Mount up." McKinley bellowed. "We move now!"

The sheriff made no attempt to deputise his lynch mob. Nor did he go through the proper channels he'd once held so dear. If they caught the outlaws, there would be no due process, just rope and feigned indignation. The sheriff disappeared into his office for a moment and came out with a double-barrelled shotgun slung over his shoulder as the posse jeered and hollered. The sheriff glanced down at the star on his chest and breathed an exacerbated sigh. He wasn't the law anymore.

McKinley climbed atop his steed, and his mob formed up around him. He slowly rode off down Main Street at the head of the haphazard column. The militia cantered through town, and as they passed Momma outside her business, the deputy shouted to her, "Don't you worry. We gone string up that n*gger boy, no two ways about it!"

McKinley heard this and glanced at his deputy in disgust. However, he knew he couldn't maintain such reservations at the head a lynching party.

The riders reached the end of Main Street, and McKinley turned and shouted to all the silent observers, "I will bring order to this goddamn desert!"

However, his face dropped as he turned away, and it became clear that not even he believed this anymore.

"Yar!" he screamed as he pushed his foot into his horse, with the rest of the riders following suit, and they went speeding off into the wastes, looking for two men who'd soon be coming from the opposite direction.

As soon as they rode out of sight, Momma and her girls sprang into action, shuffling into the street and carrying out bundles of rope between them. While one end was left around the side of the bordello, the other end was run across to the alleyway opposite, where it was tied to anything that looked sturdy enough to take the weight. At the same time, a separate team of women followed the rope and dug small trenches with trowels.

After the rope had been laid in the ditches, they began to follow along the length of them and kick dirt over them to conceal them. Momma walked over to the doctor's surgery opposite clutching a crowbar and ordered him to clear out. He protested. However Momma was in no mood to negotiate. She simply shoved his doctor's bag into his chest and said, "Don't leave this behind. You'll need it later."

Momma paced back outside and said to one of the girls, "Would you kindly fetch me some dynamite and a lever from the basement, dear?"

She responded, "What the hell are you plannin', Momma?"

"Fire and fuckin' brimstone!" Momma replied as a smirk graced her face.

Momma grunted as she lowered to one knee and began to tear up the first few floorboards outside the doctor's office. The girl came out with dynamite and a plunger in hand and a long wire draping behind her. She carefully placed the equipment down beside Momma, who began to wire the dynamite.

Momma slowly lowered the bundle of red sticks down below the floorboards and then carefully laid the boards back in place and stomped them back down. She led the wire across the street and set up the plunger, tracing back her path to bury the wire.

While the women constructed only limited cover on the ground so as to avoid suspicion, they pilled up sandbags on the roof, which were propped up behind the short wooden wall that ran along its perimeter.

After about a half an hour of setting up in the scorching morning sun, she saw a figure riding in from the north. While initially glad, as the silhouette came to a stop outside the bank, she became furious as two men climbed off the single horse.

Across town, the men could see Momma staring them down. However, by this point, it didn't really matter whether she was on board or not. William took some dynamite from the saddlebag and handed it to Tommy, who looked apprehensive. "Shouldn't we have bandannas or somethin'?" he asked.

"Maybe for style." William smirked. "But there ain't a person in town who won't know this is us."

"I guess so."

"When we go in, you rig the sticks and I'll control the teller. After everyone's been cleared, I'll meet up with Momma, and you can finish up in the vault," William explained. "We ready?" he asked one final time.

"Ready!" Tommy replied confidently.

As the men approached the bank doors, they glanced at each other one final time, and Tommy said, half sarcastically, "You sure about those masks?"

William chuckled. "You're the only black man in town. How big a mask we talkin'?"

Tommy smiled, and they unholstered their weapons. They gave the final nod before kicking open the bank doors. The room was empty save for a shaky old teller behind a wooden counter.

The teller's hands almost immediately reached under the desk. However, William rushed toward him and raised Cavanaugh's revolver to his face, shouting, "You move another inch towards that gun, and I'll kill you where you stand!" He tried to sound menacing, while desperately hoping the old man didn't call his bluff.

The teller slowly raised his hands, and William said, "OK. Now three steps back."

The old man complied immediately as he stared down the barrel of the pistol.

William smiled and said, "With an attitude like that, we'll be outta your hair in no time."

William kept his gun fixed on the old man as he slowly walked over to the door to his booth and pushed it open. He picked up the shotgun propped on top of a crate at knee height. William grinned and said, "Squirrely old bastard damn near had my legs off."

"Damn shame, to!" the teller replied with vitriol in his voice.

William smiled at the old man before shouting to Tommy, "How are things goin' back there, kid?"

"Good," Tommy shouted back. "She's almost ready to blow."

"Do we need this fool?" William asked.

"Nope. You can send him on his way." he replied.

William turned to the teller, who quaked in fear, and said to him, "You heard the man."

The teller began to blubber as he misinterpreted what was being said, "Please don't kill me, I won't tell a soul, I swear!"

"I ain't gonna kill you. Now run along and tell the sheriff for Christ's sake!" William said.

The old man was hesitant at first, but William shouted, "Go on! You don't want us to get away now do ya?"

The old man asked, confused, "You want me to what?"

"Go, you old fool, before I change my mind!" William shouted.

The teller shambled outside, wiping his tears away.

William screamed after him, "Run!"

William smirked as the teller ran away. He grabbed a few bags and paced over to Tommy, who was fixing dynamite to the last of four safes.

"Looks like we're ready," Tommy said as he took a book of matches from his pocket. "I got it. Don't you worry about me, Will." he added assertively.

Handing Tommy the bag, William said, "I'll go find Momma. When you're done here, you get outta town and find Tilly. Don't come back for hell nor high water, ya hear!"

William laid the shotgun at the doorway to the safes. "If anyone tries to stop you leavin', you put two fuckin' holes in 'em; no questions asked." he added as he turned to leave.

"Good luck, Will. Don't do anything stupid." Tommy shouted after him.

"I don't know about all that. Stupid's done all right for me so far," William replied as he paced out the bank.

He stormed out with a blind confidence that could only come from several close brushes with death, a heap load of adrenaline, and a complete disregard for considering the gravity of his situation. Yet though he still believed there would be a quick fight and a quicker payday, William was not out of his mind. He knew he may well die, just as he had known a thousand times these past few days. He had come to terms with his own mortality once on the back of that horse and then again that sleepless night on the ridge.

His death was not what troubled him. What troubled him in that moment was the knowledge that good people who didn't start this story with a death sentence may well end up with one. It didn't seem right for these people to suffer for the ambitions of a dying man. It was far too late to call off the plan. But he would happily die before letting any of these people take a bullet meant for him.

That was the man who left that bank—a man with an acute sense that his time was up, a man whose only aim now was to make sure Tommy's time was long and happy after this. Morbid as his thoughts were, he couldn't help but smile as he passed the sheriff's office and saw the old teller looking at the empty desk. He waved at the man through the sheriff's open door, and the man immediately sprinted out the back, screaming as he ran.

As William walked towards Momma, he heard an almighty bang

behind him, and the vibrations in the earth almost buckled his knees. William turned and smiled as a puff of faint smoke seeped out the bank's shattered windows. He took a moment to marvel before continuing.

When he made eyes contact with Momma, she scowled at him and silently seethed with rage. She stormed over to him. William tried desperately to think of what to say. But before he could speak, she wound up and slapped him across the face. "What the hell were you thinkin' boy! You brought a child into a battlefield to do a job we could well do ourselves!" she screamed as William hung his head and clutched the side of his face.

His cheek began to glow red, and with a ringing in one ear and screaming in the other, William tried to explain. "He wanted to come," William said cautiously. "Said he couldn't just sit back and watch."

Momma seized up as she resisted the urge to slap William again. She shouted, "You wanna put that boy's life at risk for no damn reason! There ain't no good argument for that!"

"Try telling him that," William said.

"Is this a joke to you, Mr Lee? Are you prepared to put that boy in harm's way because of our mistakes?" Momma shouted in a baffled tone as she attempted to storm away.

"Look, Momma. I know it probably wasn't wise. But he's the only one of us with explosives training. He's gonna get the money and leave straight away. He'll meet Tilly outside town just like we planned. He'll be far enough from the action to escape, with enough money to get farther still if things go wrong." William explained.

Momma stopped in her tracks and turned to look at William, still filled with an unexplainable fury.

William said, "I'm sorry, Momma, but there just ain't an outcome where Tommy passively sits on the sidelines. He just won't allow it." Momma seemed unmoved by this as William added, "Look, I'll be worrying about him as well. But he'll be OK."

Momma paced back towards him again and slapped William across the face once more. Her ring left an indent in the side of his face and knocked his wobbling tooth out. William clutched his cheek and spat his bloody tooth into the dried sand.

Momma said, in a tone far quieter than her previous level but far more threatening, "How dare you! I raised that boy. I protected that boy. I fuckin' delivered that boy! You can't even imagine the worry I feel as I send my family to fight yo battles. My daughters fight and bleed for you. My son almost got lynched for you. And you have the nerve to say that you're worried about him! Now you can rationalise it however you want, but you could've stopped him from coming here. But you didn't because it made things easier for you! Remember that when this thing goes down."

William was utterly speechless. He attempted to string a sentence together, but Momma was having none of it. "Enough! Go get a rifle from the bordello. We don't have long." Momma said, refusing to look at him.

William complied and began walking towards the bordello. He took one last look at Momma, who was staring intently at the bank, waiting for some confirmation that Tommy got out. As she saw him mount up and ride away from this sorry place, an intense relief filled her. She was finally able to think and breathe again.

William ran inside and grabbed a repeating rifle from a large crate on the bordello floor. As he came back out, he saw Momma crouching behind a small wooden barricade just to the right of the bordello porch.

She shouted to him, "You'll be down here with me, Mr Lee."

As William approached, Momma said, "Now listen up. The girls who can fight will be on the roof, but I've told them to not draw too much attention to themselves and wait for us to start the shootin'. We'll be takin' most of the heat, but I've laid a few traps that should give us the upper hand."

"You think we'll be able to manage that with just us two?" William asked nervously.

"I think we might. But those girls have enough bullets to last all night, so I've complete confidence they'll survive this thing even if we don't." Momma asserted, giving William some comfort.

"But you think we won't?" William said as his earlier adrenaline began to fade slightly.

As she watched beads of sweat begin to from on William's face, Momma said, "There ain't no knowin' how things will turn out. But if you saw the preparation that went into this, then I'm sure you'd agree that the odds are in our favour. That being said, if it's just me and you who die today, then I'll count that as a win. We live and die by our plan, son. Just have faith in it and hope for the best."

William gulped and crouched behind their small rampart. He eyed up the splintered barrels and the small planks propped against them, wondering if it would really be enough. This waist-high defence would be all that stood between them and a hail of bullets, and William couldn't help but ask, "You sure this will be good enough cover. It don't look too strong?"

Momma replied frustratedly, "It will be more than enough. Those barrels are full of sand. They'll stop anything those boys'll be carryin'!"

"Well excuse me, I didn't know these was sand barrels," William sarcastically replied.

"I've fought off hundreds of Navajo behind barricades like these. So, I'm sure they'll be more than sufficient. Why don't you just stop being such an asshole and appreciate how much we've stuck our necks out for you?" Momma snapped.

William protested, "Well I sure as hell stuck my neck out for you to deal with Thompson."

"You gave a woman beater a shit bath and now you want a fuckin' medal." Momma said dismissively.

"Well … that ain't …" William stuttered.

"I'm beginnin' to wonder if you plan on doin' any killin' on this quest for vengeance or if you just want Fortner to shoot himself." Momma interrupted as she sniggered slightly. However, she saw William looked stern and anxious. Her face straightened and she continued. "OK, son. I can't believe I'm askin' this in the position we're in. But you ever … err … shot anybody before?"

"Nothin' bigger than a deer. I can shoot. I just don't know if I'm a … a killer," William said hesitantly.

"We ain't really killers, Mr Lee. Those men out there are the killers. They're men who beat and burn and murder to their hearts' content with nobody to stop them. If we didn't do the things we do, then they would bear down on us until we broke. We are not them. We're survivors, William, plain and simple."

William seemed far less in his own head after Momma's words. However, this did nothing to stave off his shaking hands.

Momma now attempted to calm the fearful outlaw. "Don't worry. We can do this. We'll have 'em by surprise and pinned in place. Hell, we might even have this won before a shot's fired. We go on my signal, and we maximise that surprise while we have it. I promise these boys will be far slower than the deer your used to." Momma said reassuringly.

William was still trembling slightly. However, he was ever so slightly more confident. "You bring those binoculars I gave you?" Momma asked.

"No, I didn't. Tommy has them."

Momma sighed momentarily before reaching up from her little rampart and pulling out her long-scoped rifle from the bordello porch. She propped it up in the gaps in the banister and surveyed the road into town, scanning for any discernible shape against the sun-scorched horizon.

Her rifle slowly drifted from side to side as she squinted. The rifle suddenly stopped moving and locked in on one distant spot. William immediately perked up and began to climb to his feet.

Momma shouted, "You seein' this, Lucy?"

William shaded his eyes with his hand as he peered out in the distance.

"Yeah, I see it." Lucy shouted from the bordello roof.

"What?" William asked, panicked.

His tired and desert-cooked eyes began to adjust. He soon saw an arrow-shaped dust cloud pointing to a few distant dots as they crested the horizon. Before he could process what, he was seeing, Momma had already pulled her rifle out and propped it up against the barrels.

As William began to sweat and shake once more, Momma shouted up for the girls on the rooftop, "Get ready and stick to my orders. Nobody gets themselves killed!"

She then immediately turned to William and placed her hands on his shoulders, firmly saying, "Look, William, I appreciate that you're scared. But you ain't much use to me like this. Now if you stave off them shakes and don't do anythin' stupid, then you may well end up with a fresh start when this is over. Keep your head low and your eyes open until then. Can you do that son?"

"Yes, I … I can," William said, no less scared but a bit more secure upon seeing Momma's confidence.

"Then let's kill us some lawmen." Momma asserted as she took her hands off William and crouched down.

She picked up a repeating rifle. The dark wood was warm and slightly faded from the unobstructed Arizona sun. She checked if it was loaded. William lifted his own rifle and did the same.

Momma took a few bullets from her jacket pocket and placed them on the dirt. "It should be fully loaded." She hesitated as she worried that she might scare William at this crucial point. "But we may well be here a while." she finally added.

William swung back the lever of his rifle, his eyes immediately shifting to those dark figures on the horizon. He had no reaction to what Momma said. In a way, it didn't affect him. William was certainly scared, make no mistake. His heart pounded so hard he could feel his pulse echoing from his temples and from his wrists as they pressed against the gun butt. Sweat budded around his forehead and along his upper lip as his mind could scarcely decide whether to flee, fight, or freeze in place. However, this was like no other fear William had felt in his life, as this was absent any emotional backing. William had almost reached a quiet acceptance of his own mortality during that long night on the ridge, so this was merely the physical response to fear without any internal terror. William, in his own mind, was already dead.

The only anxiety he now possessed was for the lives of all the people he had dragged to this point. These were the only decent folk for miles, and William may well get them all killed. As the silhouettes sped closer, he began to dwell on the world he may leave behind after he's gone, a world noticeably worse off than before.

But it was too late for all that now. All he could do was fight to avoid the grave he had dug for them. Momma had tensely watched how William was reacting. However, she was reassured as she saw a confident look conquer his face. His hands clamped tightly around his weapon.

Momma also turned to the riding party and felt a similar rush of adrenaline as twelve angry horsemen came clearly into view. They drove furiously back towards the town, desperate to satisfy their, so far, unquenched bloodlust.

Following dark grey streams of smoke that snaked from the bank windows, McKinley and his pack rode like men possessed. Speeding past that splintery old sign, the mob entered town and disturbed that tense and serene silence. A few of the men shouted and jeered as they approached, but the words were difficult to make out over the noise of a dozen horses at full speed.

Some of the townsfolk tried to warn the men as they powered past. They shouted for them to turn back from open windows or shook heads and waved arms. Yet it was hopeless; nothing could be heard, and nothing could be done.

Momma hovered above the dynamite plunger, tensely waiting to give the signal. As this happened, the sheriff and his men buried their feet deeper into their mounts as they stormed forwards. Some screamed like berserkers as they careened down Main Street.

Above all this commotion, the sheriff heard the faintest of shouts as he approached the bordello. In the flash of an eye, a thick rope sprung from the earth and kicked up a thin curtain of dust, which fell either side of it. He may not have fully realised the danger of this situation, but his horse did. It desperately tried to avoid this obstacle just a few feet in front. Before the beast could begin to turn, its legs smashed into the tightly strung rope with enough force to send McKinley flying, flipping, and tumbling to a halt.

The rope was pulled looser, and the women holding it had been yanked forward with their arms nearly pulled from their sockets. But they were just barely able to anchor themselves and the rope in place and soon retightened the slack. The men behind him were not able to swerve in time and flew sideways over the rope as their horse hit it at an angle.

This initial carnage kicked up a huge wall of dust at the head of the column, which would gradually envelop the whole group. Those towards the back of the formation would barely manage to rip back their reins, grinding to a desperate halt as their horses pushed all four hooves into the dirt.

Momma smiled like a proud composer watching her piece performed. And now for the crescendo. She leaned on the plunger and pushed it into place. Not more than a moment later, the stairs of the doctor's surgery erupted in a thunderous cloud of wood and smoke.

Immediately after the horses skidded to a stop, most bucked up and scattered into the desert. Some carried their riders with them as they fled down alleys or turned tail completely. As the last of the horses broke for the hills, a second rope jumped up behind the men to pen them in completely.

Momma and William sprung from their cover and poured forth fire upon the confused crowd. The women on the roof followed suit and sent sporadic and targeted volleys down into the group. The smoke and dust obscured all. Picking off the men was like shooting cans in a dust storm. The only way to guarantee a hit was to fire until they saw it fall.

The confused and disoriented men clambered for cover without any real idea of where the shooters were. Those lucky enough to have kept hold of their weapons shot wildly at spectres in the fog. They aimed more based off noise than sight and rarely got close.

William must've cocked his rifle three or four times before he actually took a shot. Some part of him was, perhaps, hoping the fighting would be over before he had to do anything. He had convinced himself he was ready for this. Why didn't he feel ready?

His brow brimmed with sweat as he stood from his position. He cautiously peered over the barricade for a moment, but nothing was visible through the fog. William zeroed in on a spot in the mayhem. Yet as the crosshairs hovered over the stumbling shape, he felt his finger almost seize up with the weight of what he was about to do.

But then his spirit left his body for one solitary moment. He remembered pretending not to hear his farther beating his mother as a boy. He remembered patiently waiting for his father to finish and then hearing those plodding footsteps approach his door. He remembered sitting on his bed and wanting to do something, wanting to stop him or hide from him or even just to check his mother was all right. But something kept him sitting there; something froze up his legs like it was freezing up his finger now.

He remembered finding his mother bleeding on the kitchen floor and sobbing beside her, incapable of helping in any way that mattered. They were just two powerless people fallen victim to the worst whims of the powerful. That was a feeling he hadn't felt in a while, a feeling he thought he'd put behind him. But he'd felt it as he'd crouched beside Abigale's body, and he'd felt it a few nights ago as he sat on that log and contemplated whether to help Tommy. He blinked, Abigale's broken jaw swinging as he shook her flashed before his eyes. He pulled the trigger. It was easier than he thought it would be.

William kept firing but wasn't sure he'd shot something until a poof of red mist became visible through the dissipating dust cloud. Something in him knew the first shot was on target. He felt it in his bones.

Some men dashed for cover between buildings or behind dead horses. But as the dust began to thin and scatter, the outlaws picked them off one by one. After what couldn't have been longer than a minute, there was no discernible resistance from the riders.

William attempted to rise from his cover. He ducked back down as a shot bit the barrel in front of him. Two more whizzed above him, and he slowly began to peek out. Momma returned fire, and William saw Fortner limping backwards. He sprayed bullets the roof and the barricade with his two revolvers.

Though pinned down by a hail of fire, Momma sprung up and let loose a sure shot that struck Fortner in his shoulder as he retreated.

Cavanaugh took this opportunity to crawl out from under a corpse and make a break for safety down a different alley. He also rained fire to cover his escape. However, William did not cower from this and instead took aim at Cavanaugh. He zeroed in on the fleeing bounty hunter, taking one long inhale before squeezing the trigger.

Just before he could shoot, a stray bullet from Cavanaugh's gun hit Momma in the chest. She stumbled back, her weapon slumping as her body reeled from the impact. William dropped his gun and forgot the escaping bounty hunter as he ran to Momma's side, catching her just as her legs began to give way.

A small wound in her right shoulder slowly soaked blood into her clothes before dribbling into the ground. "She's hit!" William screamed to the girls on the roof, who began to panic and murmur.

William lifted the old woman and carried her around the back of the bordello. He booted open the door and staggered through it with Momma in his arms. The girls who'd held the ropes followed him inside in utter shock. They desperately swept the glasses and ashtrays from a table, and William laid her down.

Girls rushed down from the roof and began to crowd around Momma, and some began to cry uncontrollably. Many of the girls kept their composure and pushed William aside. They began gathering alcohol and bandages from a prepared box behind the bar. Miss Lucy surged forward and wrapped a towel around her hand before firmly pushing it onto Momma's wound. One of the girls rushed forward with a needle of morphine and stuck it into Momma's arm.

"What should I do?" William asked desperately.

"We're prepared for this, cowboy. Go do what you came for!"

Swallowing a wave of guilt and fear, William took a rifle and inhaled deeply before turning to leave. As he pushed open the swinging bordello doors, he was immediately struck by the carnage that lay before him. The thick fog had been scattered by marauding winds.

Among the smouldering wood and scattered shotguns, seven men lay dead on the ground while one more lay unconscious.

As the guns fell silent, the streets followed suit. Not a soul dared provoke their violent insurrection. William felt every eye in town on him as strode into the street. Every eye in town flinched as he suddenly turned to his right and raised his weapon. William zeroed in on movement. However, when he saw it was merely a wounded man crawling away, he slowly lowered his barrel.

Frozen in place as he raised his head, the outlaw was shocked to see Tommy riding south down Main Street. "What the hell are you doin' here kid?" William exclaimed, and his words sliced clearly through the still silence.

Tommy galloped to a halt beside William and said, "I heard the gunshots and thought I'd come help." Tommy glanced around the mayhem they'd made of Main Street. "Though it seems ya'll had it covered without me."

William looked sternly at him and shouted, "Why in the hell would you ride towards the gunshots? You goddamn idiot!"

"Look how far it's gotten you, Will!" Tommy joked, though William didn't find it funny. He continued. "Calm down, cowpoke. Tilly has the money outside town in a safe spot. Everything is gonna be just—"

"Put your fuckin' hands where I can see 'em, or I swear I'll kill you both!" a voice screamed from behind Tommy.

The men turned to see Sheriff McKinley limping towards them. He dragged his broken left leg through the dirt as he stumbled forward. The remnants of his strength could barely raise his shotgun to waist height on the outlaws. Staggering and wheezing, the sheriff shuffled sideways so he could lean on a post and take weight off his shattered leg. Dust cascaded from his once black trench coat as he fell against the small wooden pillar and used it for support. The sheriff coughed up dirt as he attempted to speak. "I ... I ain't gonna ask again!"

Tommy was unarmed and in no mood to get shot unjustly, so he raised his hands immediate and slowly dismounted his horse.

William stared the sheriff down for a few moments before finally placing his gun on the ground.

"What on earth were you boys thinkin'?" the sheriff exclaimed.

"We were just defendin' ourselves, Sheriff. I suppose that make us better lawmen then you and your lynch mob!" Tommy snarled as he looked down at this weak man.

The sheriff went to speak, but William interrupted. "So, are you gonna come to us and arrest us or do you want us to come over to your post?" William sniggered at the stern and mildly concussed sheriff.

Tommy spat to the side in disgust, and as it hit the ground, Momma heaved open the bordello door, holding a pistol in one hand and a blood-soaked towel to her shoulder with the other. She stumbled forward and raised her pistol to the sheriff with her shaking hands. A few drops of blood, which had trickled down her arm, began to drip from the gun butt as she raised the weapon.

The sheriff marvelled at this elderly woman as she began to speak. "Come now, Sheriff. No need to make a scene!" she said in a clearly weakened but still formidable tone.

"Look around you at all the folk you hurt! You think I can just let you walk away?" the sheriff desperately shouted.

"Or you could walk away!" Momma shouted back. "Take a long hard look around your feet, sheriff. Do these men represent the law you strive for? Has anything you've let them do these past days felt just to you?" Momma bellowed with one of her few remaining breaths.

The sheriff looked around him. The bodies of those around him were not good men. They were fuelled by hatred and loyal to little. Many of these men were guilty of unthinkable crimes. The sheriff had silently prayed for their incarceration, only to watch as the courts failed, and as he himself failed.

He had been deceived into believing they had similar visions for the world, yet these men who lay dead around him wanted order without law and peace absent justice. McKinley looked down at the blood and dirt and ash that had for so long clung to the underside of his fingernails.

As he glanced down, he saw a poster trapped beneath a Klansman's corpse. The top corner of the poster was burnt but he could read it clear as day: "Vote Waylon McKinley for Sheriff. He'll Fight for a Brighter Tomorrow!" The sheriff slowly lowered his weapon.

William seized this opportunity and reached for his own gun. However, he heard the muffled clank of McKinley's shotgun as it hit the ground.

Without a word, the sheriff turned and shuffled off into the desert, abandoning the town he'd once truly thought he could save. Momma couldn't help but smile as this man who'd had all his ideals beaten from him finally stood for something again. The lawman dropped his star in the sand, limped over to someone else's horse, and slowly swung his leg over the beast's back. Waylon McKinley rode like hell towards somewhere better. And who knows? Maybe he found it.

Now that he was free to do so without being shot, Tommy looked over at Momma and became overwhelmed with emotions. "What happened, Momma?" he asked desperately.

"It's just a minor wound, son. I've walked off worse than this." Momma said confidently, unwilling to share with Tommy the truth she'd already arrived upon—she was dying. Momma tried to change the subject and turned to William. "You need to go, Mr Lee. We don't have time to spare."

"She's right," William said confidently as he climbed atop the horse Tommy had ridden in.

"Not so fast. I'm comin' too." Tommy asserted.

"No, you ain't." William replied.

"Yes, I am! I've got about as much right to play a role in this as you do." Tommy said.

William looked at Momma as if expecting her to shut Tommy down. However, Momma didn't say anything. Tommy was here now anyway, and she wanted to spare him the pain of seeing her die. "Just don't get yourselves killed." she finally said, exhausted, before hobbling back inside to finish being bandaged up.

The outlaws trotted down the alley Fortner had initially sprinted down. His footprints were the only fresh ones. They trailed along them, occasionally seeing patches of wet blood on the floor or a partial scarlet handprint on a fence. They emerged from the alley and dashed south, slowing down every so often to check they were still on the right track.

The men caught sight of Fortner as they galloped towards the cliff. He had passed the point of being able to walk unaided and now shifted along the cliff and held himself up with it when necessary. Blood drenched his shirt and sleeve, and the scar on his face was accompanied by a deep gash on his forehead. A thick torrent of blood dribbled down his face.

When he heard hooves approaching, Fortner simply fell against the cliff and sat in place. William dismounted and strode towards the disarmed man while Tommy followed behind him with a cold and imperious stare.

As Fortner painfully reached into his pocket, William shouted, "What are you doing?"

But the man took little notice and pulled a cigarette from a packet.

He finally looked up at the outlaws who would be his end. He wryly smirked and said, "No wonder we couldn't catch you. That poster looks nothin' like ya!" He began to laugh but soon clutched his gun wound, as it seared with pain. "One hell of a show you boys put together back there." He finally got a now bloody match to burn and lit his last cigarette. "Almost impressive." he added.

"It was mostly Momma's doin'," Tommy said.

"I can't say I'm surprised; this fool doesn't exactly look like a criminal mastermind." Fortner said as he gestured to William.

William pushed his gun barrel into Fortner's cheek. "You know a girl called Abigale Lee?" he snarled.

"No. Can't say I do." Fortner said in a remarkably calm tone.

William pulled the barrel away and beat him into the dirt with the gun butt. As he lay desperate and wheezing on the ground, William pushed once more into his cheek with the barrel. "So you're tellin' me you don't know nothin' about a murder out near Falcon Falls?" William shouted at the man as he spat up puddles of blood.

"What that Navajo girl? Cavanaugh killed her, son. He's always had a thing for savage girls. But the way he told it, she wasn't too keen on him," Fortner calmly explained. "Is that what all this has been about?"

"Don't you lie to me, you son of a bitch!" William screamed as his gun barrel burrowed into Fortner's temple. "It was your name in that bordello logbook!"

"What fuckin' logbook?" Fortner shouted.

"Mommas logbook! I found a room key at our house the night she was killed, a room key rented out in your fuckin' name." William screamed, his shouts reflecting off the cliff and echoing in the distance.

"Momma's logbook?" Fortner said as he shook his head slowly. He began to chuckle to himself.

This enraged William, who struck Fortner across the face before shouting. "What?"

Fortner groaned painfully before continuing. "She played you, son. She played you like a fuckin' fiddle."

"Bullshit!" William screamed as he pinned Fortner's head up against the cliff.

"So, you saw this logbook with your own eyes then?" Fortner asked, and he got his answer as he felt William relieve the pressure on his head slightly. He continued, "Not a soul leaves that shithole without Momma takin' note, and she knows Cavanaugh was out on business out past Falcon Falls. But she sent you after me—a man she knew you couldn't reach without shootin' half the town to shit."

"But it was my idea to stage an ambush, my idea to rob the bank!" William desperately rationalised.

"And she'd just happened to have the dynamite ready. I bet she would've hit that bank regardless, and I bet she couldn't believe her luck when you offered to do that for her as well." Fortner explained. "Face it, kid. If you was after the man who killed Abigale, you should've finished him out in the desert!"

William tensed up and contemplated just shooting the man regardless, but he had other priorities now. It seemed he was following the wrong set of tracks. As he relieved the pressure on Fortner's skull, the man began to writhe on the ground. William turned and began to walk back over to his horse, and Fortner mumbled to himself through mouthfuls of blood, "All this for some redskin whore!"

Fortner rolled over and revealed a revolver tucked in his waist. As Fortner raised the weapon to William, Tommy shot the man without hesitation. William was startled and turned to see Tommy looming over a headless corpse, his barrel smouldering and smoking as he lowered it.

Fortner's brain matter painted the cliff face and trickled over his limp body; his blood dried quick in the mid-day sun.

William had imagined this moment a thousand times, and Tommy had imagined it a million, yet it gave neither the satisfaction they'd hoped for. It brought neither closure nor completion, just a faint nausea as they watched blood spirt from Fortner's opened cranium and slowly dribble dry. The men sat in complete silence, observing the consequences of their crusade.

Far-off gun shots cut through their contemplation, and the outlaws began to mount up. They said nothing on their hasty ride back to town. They were almost relieved that something sprung up to distract them from their guilt and disappointment. The men would chase any opportunity to temporarily forget the sensation of Fortner's very being pooling up in cracks in the soil.

William wasn't certain what Tommy saw in the moment he snuffed out a life. From his own experience, he could only imagine he saw the body of his father as it dangled in the distance. He didn't know how hard it was for Tommy to kill Fortner, but he could only imagine it was easier than the boy had thought it would be.

CHAPTER 14

Rest for the Wicked

Momma lay dying on the cold whisky-stained, table. The pain she felt, and the opioids she'd been given battled in her bloodstream. She gazed up at the ornate patterns that swirled along the bordello ceiling. The patterns in the centre of her field of view began to shift and snake, while those in the periphery blurred in and out of focus. Her heartbeat grew quicker and weaker. She felt every agonising pound upon her chest. Her skin had turned grey and sweaty. Her lips were corpse blue. Her eyelids dropped low and heavy.

Momma's consciousness rattled about in her failing body. She was confused and gripped by an intense anxiety. She couldn't look at the ceiling patterns, as her dizzying mind desperately searched for solid ground. Every sensation came at once to her collapsing mind, a powerful and pervasive nausea, a weakening drumbeat in her chest, a distracting and overwhelming thirst.

Tilly crept in the back door and quietly asked, "Is it over?"

Her family all crowded around something, but she couldn't see what.

Tilly tensely moved closer to the table. Momma stretched across it. She pushed through the huddled women and began to weep at Momma's side. The old woman looked up at her with recognition in her eyes. Tilly desperately asked what had happened, but Momma couldn't hear anything over her dampened heartbeat and the rippling pulse it caused in her body.

She lacked the ability to speak or to comprehend speech, yet she still saw. She saw, crowded around her, a family she once believed she was undeserving of. Momma felt confused and fatigued and so cold. As Tilly rested her head on Momma's arm, her blue lips curved to a contented smile.

Those overwhelming sensations began to weaken now, her thirst distracted her less, and her nausea was less overwhelming. That accelerating heartbeat dulled and dampened as if someone were smothering a snare drum with a pillow. Bellowing stimuli gave way to serene silence, silence and the sensation of oblivion. A part of her was glad the noise was stopping; a part of her was just tired. Yet there is no rest for the wicked.

A shaken voice echoed from the street outside. "Your luck ends here, outlaw! You and the boy best come out now and die like men!"

This sparked something in Momma, maybe not life but an echo of it—a tug upon her last tether to this world. Pulled from the abyss for just a few moments longer, she summoned the strength to somehow move. She stumbled forward as Tilly tried to restrain her. But in the last moments of her life—just as in every other moment of her life—there wasn't much that could hold Momma back.

She brushed past those in her path but stopped just in front of the door as she felt Tilly's hand on her shoulder. Momma turned around, and Tilly almost wept as her translucent fingers wrapped around her hand. "Don't go out there, Momma!" Tilly pleaded.

Momma calmly replied, "You girls take care of each other. We're all we got." And with that, she let go of Tilly's hand and turned around again.

She almost fell through the door in an attempt to push it open yet strode out onto the bordello porch with a confidence only brought about by severe blood loss. Her gaze was unfocussed and almost empty as she scanned for any shape in blinding sunlight. She took comfort in the warm embrace of the sun. Momma found peace in the heat; she'd felt so cold before. That arid sun that had done nothing but make her sweat, blister, and wrinkle for decades now washed over her like a gift from God, the final comfort offered to a dying woman.

Cavanaugh watched her from the saloon roof through the scope of a long rifle. He scanned up and down this pale and delirious shadow as she stood still in the open with no regard for her surroundings.

As he focused the cross hairs on her body, he saw the large and freshly reopened wound on her torso. Even from this distance, he could see she was dying. And more than that, he could see from her expression that she had made some peace with it. Cavanaugh felt no such peace at his own demise, he wanted to take it from her.

He hovered the cross hairs over her torso and squeezed the trigger. The shot cracked the air, and Momma crimpled from the impact. She was dead before she hit the ground; in a way, she was dead before she ever got off that table. Cavanaugh cocked back the bolt once again and fired two additional shots into her limp corpse. A smug smile pulled at the edge of his mouth; he could almost hear the bullets tearing into her skin.

CHAPTER 15

A Breath Unhindered

William and Tommy powered towards town in complete silence and blissful ignorance. The dangling sign on the way into Temperance teetered as the outlaws sped past. Everything seemed to be where they left it, save for an extra body on the bordello steps. Tommy squinted at it as William rode; however, both were interrupted by a deafening bang.

William saw a faint flash on the saloon roof before his eyes immediately darted down at his horse. Cavanaugh's shot struck the beast in the jaw, and it tumbled and folded beneath the weight of the men, who flew forward into the street.

William was disorientated and terrified, and he simply sat in the dirt for a few seconds as he processed his panic. Tommy ran forward and shoved the outlaw into an alley, tumbling after him. As Tommy fell forward, a shot nipped the ground behind him and spat dirt at his heels.

William fell into the mud of the alley, still panicked and somewhat unaware. He gasped and glimpsed around for a few moments until Tommy's voice finally became audible above his thundering pulse and tightening chest. "Focus, Will!" Tommy shouted frustratedly.

William finally showed recognition, and Tommy continued. "Did you see where he was?"

"Er ... the ... the saloon roof I think." William replied to Tommy's relief.

However, this relief faded. "He has a clear view of every way out. We sure as hell won't find cover out there!" he exclaimed, gesturing to the featureless desert. "We need to dislodge him somehow."

A bullet struck the corner of the wooden building they cowered behind; it sprayed fragments and splinters next to them. This seemed to bring William fully back to reality.

Tommy looked back at him—as he attempted to bring down his frantic breathing—and said, "Do you have your gun?"

William nodded as he yanked it from his waistband.

"That makes one of us." Tommy glanced at his new shotgun in the dead centre of main street.

William, dusty and still somewhat disoriented, finally spoke. "Dynamite!" he said as his eyes focused. "I bet Momma's got some dynamite left. Do you think we could throw some up there?"

"Maybe," Tommy replied. He shifted closer to the edge of the building, waited for Cavanaugh to shoot, and then swiftly swung his head around to pin down the bounty hunter's location. As he yanked his head back to safety, a bullet whizzed just past him and spat wood onto his lap.

Tommy took a moment of contemplation as he brushed the splinter off. He seemed to find a new confidence within himself; after all, they were dead men anyway. "I can get it up there!" Tommy asserted. "If you can help me get there, I can get it done."

This bravado seemed to flow into William and help him to finally kick his shakes. He nodded firmly and said, "Let's do this!"

Tommy took one final peek out, whipping his head back to dodge the hail of fire that followed. "All right then. I think I can make it to the back of the bordello if I stay low. When you see me go in, you count out two minutes. Lay down some cover fire, and I should be able to make it to the saloon. Don't poke your head out. Don't get yourself killed. Just make noise!" Tommy said.

"Sounds good, Tommy," William said. "Hell! You're better at this than I am."

"That ain't no secret, cowpoke." Tommy joked.

Laughing for a moment, William extended his hand, and Tommy shook it. "Good luck, Tommy!" he said warmly.

"You too, Will!" he replied.

Tommy broke away and began to sneak around the back of the building.

He cautiously moved across the alley towards the bordello. William poked his head around and watched as Tommy approached the bordello's back steps. He slowly went up them before stopping at the door.

The outlaws made eye contact, and Tommy counted out on his fingers—three, two, one. And with that, he pushed open the door, and the cowboys began counting in unison. William, keeping a steady count in his head, loosed a few blind shots at Cavanaugh to let him know they were still there. William then took a step back from the edge and let Cavanaugh send his reply. He calmly emptied his cylinder and reloaded. Thirty seconds.

Everyone in the bordello shuddered as Tommy pushed open the back door. Those women had heard nothing but gunshots and mayhem; one can see why they'd assume it was the reaper at the door. Many of them sighed with much-needed relief as they saw Tommy alive, but their faces soon dropped as they saw the cocky look on his face. Tommy didn't know she was dead.

He powered towards the basement hatch, murmuring numbers as he went. He heaved open the hatch and sped down. He rooted around among a few red crates before finding a couple of loose dynamite sticks. He desperately continued looking around and found a lighter among some other junk. He turned to climb out from the basement. One minute.

Tommy climbed out, and immediately Tilly stepped into his path. "Why the hell did you come back here, Tommy?" she shouted.

"Because I had to, Till" Tommy said as he attempted to sidestep her and move towards the door.

"You didn't, Tommy." she shouted as she followed him. "You still don't! This just ain't you."

Tommy turned to her, subconsciously still counting away. He placed his hands on her arms and looked her in the eyes. His mere touch put her at ease. He said, "This is just what needs to be done, Till. You know what momma always says, People gotta adapt sometimes."

One minute thirty seconds.

Tommy kissed he her on the forehead. She grabbed his hand as he attempted to pull away. Teary-eyed, she said softly to him "Find me when this is all over."

Tommy's thumb gently stroked her hand as his lips formed a warm smile that cut through her soul. "I'll find you."

Tilly finally let go of his hand, and Tommy turned to face the door. The two minutes was almost up. In perfect unison, twenty feet apart, the outlaws counted.

Five, Tommy flicked his lighter to check it worked. Four, William made the sign of the cross on his heathen chest. Three, Tommy gave Tilly one last glance as he rested his hand on the door handle. Two, William pulled back his pistol hammer and shuffled towards the edge of the building. One, the outlaws closed their eyes and took a deep breath.

Tommy swung open the bordello door and ran for his life, every sound around him faded to white noise. Everything in his periphery blurred and blackened. The only thing clear to him in that moment was the focal point of his vision and his only objective, the saloon.

William swung his arm out and fired two shots in Cavanaugh's vague direction. On the third shot, he poked his head around to see the outline of Cavanaugh's rifle drifting towards Tommy.

As Tommy ran through the open range of Main Street and Cavanaugh took aim, he realised he had but one choice. William stood from his cover and openly strode toward Cavanaugh, whizzing shots past the bounty hunter, which got his attention. Cavanaugh's rifle drifted back to William, and its scope flashed in the Arizona sun.

William couldn't help but find peace as he gazed down the barrel. After all, he was a dead man already, a dead man who'd finally found something worth dying for.

Cavanaugh found no great enlightenment on his side of the rifle, just the same cold emptiness that filled him every time he took a life. He squeezed the trigger and watched as the outlaw's chest absorbed the shock. William stumbled to a halt and slowly fell to his knees, dropping his pistol in the dirt. Cavanaugh quickly yanked back the bolt and put another shot in his right shoulder. His lip twitched faintly, and he pulled back the bolt. Two down, one to go.

Tommy, who could hardly hear the noise over his pulsing adrenaline, kept running. A spent shell pinged past Cavanaugh's head as he darted his rifle down. He was hot on Tommy's heels as he sprinted to the saloon. However, Tommy made it close enough to the saloon to block Butch's shot.

Tommy gasped, as he wrestled with his raging heartbeat. He fell to one knee and desperately tried to work the lighter in his sweaty hands.

Finally coaxing a flame from the thing, Tommy held it to the fuse of the dynamite. The top of the red stick began to sparkle and burn, and Tommy took a deep breath. He stood up and, while facing the saloon doors, began to slowly step backwards. When he believed he was far enough back to make the shot, Tommy launched the stick up and forwards, clenching his whole body in anticipation of the stick falling back down on him.

As Cavanaugh scanned the periphery of his blind spot beneath him for any sign of Tommy, he heard a hissing pass his head. The bounty hunter took little notice initially as he saw Tommy sprinting away. Halfway through taking aim, Cavanaugh realised why he was running. He dropped his rifle as he lunged for the stick. Its hissing reached a crescendo. The bounty hunter and the saloon roof went up in a puff of smoke, and their remains scattered the streets of Temperance.

Tommy fell and ducked as he heard the explosion, clutching his head in his hands. For a few seconds after, he just waited there. Waited for the adrenaline to wear off so he could tell if he'd been shot. Waited for a smouldering plank to knock him dead. Waited for his life to end as he so surely expected it would. But Tommy wasn't dead, and his body soon unclenched, and he clambered to his feet.

He turned to the crumbling saloon, its roof and the top of its walls shredded to planks and strewn about town. Tommy took no joy in what he'd done, but he would do it all again in a heartbeat. For all it had cost, Tommy knew that liberation from this place was within grasp. Unfortunately, Tommy would soon learn the full scope of what this had cost.

Tommy turned around as the girls filtered into the street. Tilly strode out onto the porch and sighed with relief to see him alive. She saw the slight smile on his face, and she watched it dissipate as he looked around.

Tommy ran over to Momma's body and desperately checked the pulse of this clearly dead woman. She was warmed by the sun, yet still colder than alive. Tommy wept at her side as he clutched onto her hand. Through the dozen tears that obscured his view, he saw the body of William not far away.

Tommy curled back up next to Momma's body as if he were still covering from the explosion. He sat in complete silence. The only noise was the faint patter of his tears as they fell to the ground and soaked into the cracked earth. He would occasionally sharply inhale as he gasped for air to fuel his weeping, but he mostly just remained completely still.

Tommy raised his head for just a moment and saw the burgundy hole between Williams shoulder blades. He was able to peer into his friend's very being, and it was nothing short of looking into a great and consuming abyss. These two people had saved his life on many occasions, yet this was a favour he was incapable of returning. What Tommy would never know was both these people would've, in their final moments, rather died a thousand times than given him the opportunity to return that favour.

He felt Tilly's hands press gently on his back, and he saw her own teary face creep into his peripheral. He felt no less empty but infinitely less alone. "We'll give them a proper burial Tom," Tilly said compassionately as she embarrassed him. "We'll bury them on the cliffside. Lord knows she hated this place, but she loved the view from up there."

Tommy eventually found the will to move from his spot, to bear the sight of his friend and the woman who'd raised him without keeling over and breaking down. They sombrely loaded the bodies onto horses, and this procession of prostitutes marched in perfect silence.

They trekked up to the ridge and found a spot near the edge beneath a great bent oak. As the others dug graves, Tilly rode off to find the money. She came back to find a crowd of women around two fresh dirt rectangles. Handmade wooden crosses rose about two feet off the ground, just high enough to peek over the cliff's edge and see the valley below. Rocks lined the boundary of the graves.

Tilly gently pushed through the crowd and saw Tommy kneeling between the mounds of earth. Tommy had sat there still for twenty minutes, and he would sit there for twenty more before he finally spoke. "Where should we go?" he said dispassionately to the dozen people who mourned around him.

"Anywhere we want, Tommy." Tilly said as she put her arm around him.

Tommy rested his head on Tilly's waist and closed his eyes in inexpressible agony. He finally let go and cried into her dress. He wrapped his arms around Tilly. "Where do we go?" Tommy asked desperately as tears streamed down his face.

Tilly unwrapped his arms from around her and crouched down to his level. She looked him right in the eyes and said firmly, "We can go anywhere in the world, Tommy—anywhere!"

The tears stopped in Tommy's eyes, more from exhaustion than from any real comfort. He smiled at Tilly and took her hand in his. He slowly turned towards the horizon and inhaled a deep breath of the freshest and cleanest air he had ever tasted, and he exhaled freely for the first time in a long time.

Maybe they would find their Zion beyond that horizon. Or maybe they would just find more ugliness and vice. But the possibilities were wider than any of these people had been offered before. Tommy looked back at Tilly and gently stroked her hand. The tear tracks on his face began to dry, and his hands began to steady. He looked her in the eyes. "Anywhere, Tilly." he said hopefully. "Anywhere we want."

CHAPTER 16

Till Death Do Us Part

I n a rarely traversed section of northern Arizona, far from all that was good and close to nothing nice, wound a forgotten track. This trail was worn and widened from a century of passing pioneers. However, this former artery now trickled dry. Along this sloping trail once flowed all the gold pulled from the cliffs of Temperance and all the greedy souls who chased it. Now this road saw nothing but coyotes, rattlesnakes, and the occasional lost traveller.

Time had forgotten the path. Agaves and cactuses began thinning the overexpanded road and pushing in on its edges with their roots. The world had left this place behind. The railroads and their expanding tendrils of civilisation had long since circumnavigated this small slice of desert. This was the only road into Temperance; however, it was not often travelled these days. Most folk have no desire to live in such squalor, with those who do often being more than happy to die in it.

Along this lonely little road was a solitary homestead. It stood at the edge of a thin and low oasis of greenery that bordered a small river. The outside of this house was, perhaps, once a light blue, yet it had since faded to grey beneath the burning sun. It had a pleasant front porch with a singular mahogany rocking chair that faced out onto the small stream.

Even in a place as harsh as this, life still bloomed. Jackrabbits, prairie dogs, and birds alike all moved up and down this stream to take one last sip of precious water before retiring for the night. And watching the sun set over all that life from her kitchen window stood Abigale Lee.

Abigale hunched over a sink full of dishes, silently watching the suds slide off each plate. She lifted each one from the hot water only to then put them back in. She would occasionally lift her head to see the beautiful scene before her. However this would only upset her as she marvelled at all this life out of her reach.

Exhausted and alone, Abigale dropped the cup she was holding into the hot soapy broth before watching it slowly be engulfed. It was a strange feeling, to feel more emotional connection to dishes in a skin than to the world or the people around you.

Abigale took a step back from the sink out of fear that one more dish may well drive her insane. She looked once more at the scene outside. Her eyes tracking a thrush as it hopped from branch to brittle branch, and as the little bird glanced round for predators, its eyes would occasionally meet Abigale's. The dainty little thrush twitched as it tried to figure out if that strange creature inside that strange tree was a threat or not. It was the first time in a long time that Abigale had really felt seen.

This moment was interrupted by a rustling in the brush, and both their eyes darted towards the disturbance. The rustling halted, almost as if deliberately stopped, and Abigale watched as the thrush fled deeper into the semi-desolate patch of woods. Abigale was strangely impacted by the thrush leaving; however, her eyes would once again focus on the origin of the rustling.

She could make out little through the twilight and the vegetation. However she could faintly see the outline of a black shape that seemed darker than its distant surroundings. This figure was on the other side of the small river and hidden between a bush and a large rock. On top of this came a strong sensation that she was being watched, a sensation no doubt shared by that little bird as it perched on that branch; if only Abigale could leave so easily.

Abigale inched forwards and squinted at the distant shape. However, by now the daylight had all but escaped across the horizon, and whatever was out there had become deathly still. A shiver strode down her spine, and a fearful spike of adrenalin began to surge around her bloodstream.

Abigale turned her head sharply to the right, her short ponytail swaying as she did so. She confidently paced over to an old drawer in her living room and yanked it open. An old neglected six-gun slid to the front of the drawer as it slumped downward. Picking up the gun, Abigale rushed outside and jumped off her porch onto the dull orange dirt. She saw movement out of the corner of her eye and began to cautiously stalk towards it. Abigale raised the pistol to hip height and slowly walked the thin path. She followed the trail as it dissected the vegetation and as it temporarily disappeared into the shallow river.

Since emerging from her house with the revolver, she had not felt the sensation of being watched, and she had seen no trace of this shadow man she was tracking. However, she soon glimpsed a significantly larger silhouette snaking down the trail in her direction. She didn't quite take aim at the figure but centred her weapon in that direction.

As the figure rounded the path's final turn, it bellowed from the darkness, "What the hell you doin', Abigale?" in a voice she recognised.

Abigale promptly lowered the gun to her side as the face of her husband, atop his Hungarian half-breed, emerged from the darkness. William trotted into view as he shouted "That ain't a goddamn toy, Abi!"

"I saw somebody movin' out here, Will. Somebody's gotta defend our home!" William sighed as Abigale added, "Where were you this time then?"

William ignored her resentful tone and impatiently said, "In town. Do you have a problem with that?"

Abigale looked up at her husband as he rode around her with an unempathetic look in his eyes. As he began to dismount, she said, "Seems like all you do these days is sneak off to work every mornin' and sneak in from town every night."

William was clearly unwilling to listen to Abigale and dismissively said, "I have things I need to do in town, and I ain't got no other time to do them."

"Don't bullshit me, Will! If you're just runnin' errands, then why can I never go with you?" she asked.

"You can't go to that place, Abigale. It's out of the question." William said bluntly.

"Why? Because it's a 'Klan town'? Or because then you'll have no place to drink and whore in peace?" Abigale shouted.

As he fiddled about with the reins, William said over his shoulder,

"It ain't like that. I'm not riskin' your life by takin' you there." He dispassionately turned and walked up the steps to the porch.

Abigale paced after William and asked, "Well why do you have to go there if it's so damn dangerous?"

"So, I can forget being trapped in this horrible scrap of country, workin' a job I hate." William said hesitantly as he pushed open his front door.

Abigale followed him, waiting for him to turn around and speak to her. She said, "Then let's just leave. I mean it ain't like you get paid enough anyway. It ain't like I've got much family left around here anymore neither. We can go west or north or any place we want, Will. we got nothing holding us down." Her tone was empathetic and caring, yet William's was not as he turned to speak to her.

"That ain't why," William began to stutter but stopped himself. "Er … it's not …" He tried again to find his words.

"What exactly is makin' you feel trapped, Will?" Abigale said, the compassion fading from her voice. As William tripped over his own tongue, she said after a tense swallow, "Do I make you feel trapped, William?"

William said nothing, and nothing was the last thing Abigale wanted to hear. She knew her husband; she could read his thoughts as if they were sprawled across his gawping face. Abigale began to well up with tears. She could no longer look at William. She threw the revolver back in its drawer and stumbled over to a bottle of whisky on the shelf. Her trembling hands poured a drink to the sound of William's deafening and brutal silence.

As she raised the glass to her lips, William finally spoke. "Look, Abi …" But the words to fix things flittered from his grasp.

"You feel trapped," she said as she turned to look at him. Her tone became more furious as she said, "I stay in this tiny wooden box for weeks on end, waiting for a husband who hates me to come home stinkin' of booze. We're far from where my family ended up, and the only town for miles is full of people who hate me." William shuddered in fear as she continued, her whisky wobbling as she seethed with rage. "But please, tell me more about how trapped you feel."

William remained unequipped to find the words to respond and said, "It's not just you, Abi."

"You barely come home. You barely speak to me. We haven't spoken in a week, and even now you just won't talk to me. I'm happy to wait all night for you to find the words you're looking for, but I just need you to tell me how you feel. Do you still love me, Will?" she said, agonising over the words as she formed them.

And once again, William said nothing. But Abigale knew what nothing meant. She was right. She finished her drink in one before turning around and leaning against the wall. "Get the fuck out, William." she said in a detached and broken tone as her gradually steadying hands poured a larger drink.

William approached her, but she simply turned away, sipping her drink imperiously. He soon realised she wasn't turning around and that he lacked the words to make her do so. He stood there for a few moments before walking away. He gathered his fishing rod and the only bottle of whisky that wasn't near his sobbing wife. He hung in the doorway a moment on his way out. "I'll be back tomorrow mornin' if you wanna talk." he said sombrely.

Abigale was going to say something to William as he left her there alone, say something about all she'd given for him and all the ways he'd disappointed her. She was going to scream at him for just leaving her there out of sheer cowardice, but she didn't. She said nothing because she owed him nothing. Abigale simply let him leave, secure in the knowledge she wouldn't be here when he got back.

In the cloud of dust her husband left behind, Abigale finally found the strength to give up. She walked back inside and began quietly packing her things. She bundled a bag full of clothes and valuables, stopping for a moment towards the end to consider if she was really willing to walk away from a house she'd spent five years as a seamstress helping to afford. But this house was nothing to her anymore. The frames on its mantle were meaningless; the memories within it were hollow. This house was little more than a cage.

As Abigale stepped out onto her porch, she immediately started crying as she realised William had taken their only horse. This cage would contain her a little longer.

Her silent despair was interrupted by a voice that said, "You all right, ma'am?" And it simultaneously bellowed with a gravelled authority and cracked nervously.

Abigale looked up to see a large man in a fine pressed suit standing at the bottom of her porch and holding his hat beside him. His hair was patchy and grey, and he had neurotically combed each hair into place. His face was clean shaven but dotted with a few patches of hair where he'd shaven in imperfect light. He had pushed a primrose through his lapel and his tie was almost perfectly central in his collar. Though his suit looked almost brand new, Abigale could see faint patched of dirt around the knees.

She cautiously eyed up the stranger as he cleared his throat to speak. "I ain't tryna intrude or nothin', ma'am. I just heard some commotion and wanted to check everything was OK," Cavanaugh said as he picked at the loose threads in his hat. His voice struck the perfect balance between meek and terrifying, and this unnerved Abigale.

Abigale politely smiled and said, "I'm all right, Mr ...?"

"Cavanaugh, ma'am!" he said like an excited pup.

"Well, Mr Cavanaugh," Abigale began as she thought of the quickest and least dangerous way out of this interaction, "I'm havin' a bit of a difficult day. So I think it might be best if I just get some sleep." She eyed him up to gauge his reaction. When she saw this didn't seem to bother him, she got up and began to carry her bag inside.

"You know, I ride past this place a lot. I don't think it's right for him to treat you the way he does." he blurted out.

Abigale turned on the spot and said angrily, "I'm sorry, sir. But I don't know you. I don't know what would give you the right to speak on my marriage."

Butch moved slightly closer to the clearly retreating woman and held out a room key as he said, "I have a place in town where you could lie low for a while. If you ever need to get away." He spoke frantically as he tried to frame himself as helpful, rather than strange and intrusive.

She scoffed at this suggestion as said, "So you find a cryin' woman and you decide to invite her into your bed?"

"No, no it's not like that. I'm just concerned for your safety. I know you ain't happy, ma'am. I see you starin' out that window every day. I could make you happy. I could make it so you don't ever have to worry about your husband again." Butch said as he held out a faded sheet of paper.

"Get the fuck off my property!" Abigale said as she turned to go inside.

She noticed Cavanaugh attempting to climb the porch behind her. As she rushed through the door, she slammed it shut behind her. The door clocked Cavanagh in the face and broke his nose with an almighty crack. However, the bounty hunter's boot stopped it from shutting completely, and it began to swing back open.

Cavanaugh's head recoiled as stepped back and clutched his nose, which swelled and obscured part of his vision. As his hands rushed to stop the two thick trails of leaking blood, he dropped the key, and it tumbled onto the porch floor. The bounty hunter recovered from his disorientation as Abigale rushed to a drawer on the far side of the room. Cavanaugh clambered after her, blood drenching his hands and chin. Abigale yanked the drawer open as the quick and heavy footsteps drew closer behind her. She picked up the revolver and frantically turned to raise it in the direction of the footsteps. Abigale closed her eyes and made a momentary prayer for her life before squeezing the trigger.

The gun jumped in her trembling hands, and her ears began to ring. A small puff of smoke obscured her vision for a moment. But as it cleared, she saw Cavanaugh lunging at her. He pushed the gun barrel aside, wincing as the hot steel seared his palm. His hand shifted from the barrel to Abigail's wrist as he forced it upward and pushed Abigale into the wall.

A fresh hole in Butch's arm began to spirt blood; it seems she hadn't missed after all. Abigale, thinking quickly, used her free hand to press down on the wound as she attempted to escape his grip.

Cavanaugh pulled his right shoulder back in pain but kept his left hand firmly around Abigale's wrist. She used this small break to beat at Cavanaugh with her left hand, aiming for his broken nose and bleeding shoulder. However, she never again landed such a painful blow.

Cavanaugh pulled back his arm and punched her in the face. As her jaw broke and her head flew sideways, her body followed suit, and she tumbled to the floor, losing grip of the gun.

Cavanaugh let her collapse as he pulled the gun from her hands. He loomed over her, nearly in tears as he stared at what he had done. "I didn't want this, Abigale. I never would've wanted this!" he said as Abigale sobbed silently and sputtered up blood.

Abigale refused to acknowledge him as her crying grew louder. Cavanaugh, unwilling to let this poor woman suffer in peace, continued,

"We could still go back, Abigale. It's not too late. We could leave here right now if you wanted!" Butch pleaded as he desperately tried to avoid finishing what he'd started.

Abigale groaned in agony as blood filled her mouth and blocked her airways. She gasped for air as she cried, coughing up blood every few moments to allow herself to breath. The pain in her face made it nearly impossible to form words, but she would for this. She raised her head, coughing up one final mouthful of blood and taking one final gasp of air before mumbling "Fuck you!" And with that, her head slumped back down, and she made her peace with God.

Cavanaugh's face seized up with enraged impotence as he realised what he—at least in his mind—had to do. There was no turning back. He centred the gun on her fidgeting body, turned his head to the side so he wouldn't have to see, and pulled the trigger three times.

What he had managed to avoid seeing he could surely taste as a thin mist of blood filled the air. Cavanaugh breathed a tortured sigh and lowered the gun, still unable to look at her. She gave one final breath before fading out of this world. Her soul left her body—a bird finally freed from its cage.

Cavanaugh felt the warmth from the barrel as it hung by his side. Smelt the smoke and the iron in the air. Heard the faint noise of splintered wood falling to the floor. The bounty hunter opened his eyes and—though a veteran of two wars and more lynchings than he could remember—damn near threw up on the spot. His trembling fingers dropped the gun. His lip began to quiver. His stomach began to churn.

Parts of her were shot into the floor, and her white blouse was soaked red in pints of blood. Though her head slumped to one side, and her shattered jaw slumped farther still, her eyes looked as peaceful as when they'd been tracking that thrush.

Cavanaugh looked down at her peaceful green eyes. If he blocked out the blood and ignored all the agony, he could almost imagine she was still alive. Butch staired into her empty eyes wondered if she had found a world more satisfying then this one in death. Maybe Butch had set her free, or maybe he was just part of a world that was dead set on taking one last thing from Abigale Lee. Maybe she found nothing in a place called nowhere, and maybe her eyes were simply the last part of her to find that out. Cavanaugh slowly pulled the primrose from his lapel and dropped it beside her body. It fell in perfect silence and settled beside her open left hand.

Butch Cavanaugh slunk off into the woods to tend to his wounds, crouching at a log he often stopped at to watch Abigale. He had come upon a home and left a wasteland in his wake. He had barged in and tried to take what he believed was his and left behind only pain. Such was the tragedy of Butch Cavanaugh.

William had just reached the river when he heard the first gunshot. He immediately turned tail and rode back to the only house for miles around. His mind raced in fearful anticipation. He grappled with every scenario save for the worst-case one, which eluded his comprehension. He dug his boots into his stallion and shook the reins with the force of cresting waves on stormy nights.

William had found himself unable to be with Abigale for reasons he lacked the emotional honesty to grapple with. He had thought of losing his marriage, but he had never once thought of truly losing his wife.

As he approached his home, he jumped from the speeding horse and sprinted up the porch. Cavanaugh watched from the woods as he finished bandaging his wound. William immediately noticed his door was ajar and swinging in the gentle wind. The door drifted shut as William approached, only to be stopped by a small key in the doorway. He picked up the key before rising to his feet and slowly pushing open the door.

William was not a man desensitised to violence; nor was he accustomed the scent of iron that hit him as the door wafted open. He saw her instantly; he didn't know whether to throw up or break down.

William rushed to her side and kneeled beside her mangled body. He gagged and hyperventilated as his eyes flooded with tears. A wave of panic throttled his breathing, and his heart pounded at his ribcage until it flexed from the force.

William couldn't contain it anymore; tears began to stream from his eyes, and he began to gag and throw up. He'd eaten nothing that day so found himself staring into a puddle of bile and whisky. After a few moments of this, he leaned back. He was no less revolted or grief-stricken yet found himself too tired to express either emotion.

William closed his eyes and looked up, delusional in the hope that prayer would undo what was done. His silent meditation was interrupted by faint footsteps outside, but William didn't move. He heard the faint creak of his door as it drifted open behind him, but William didn't turn around. He heard the faint whizzing of rusty spurs as they crept up behind him, but William didn't care.

Those footsteps grew louder as they marched towards him. On another day, William may have jumped to his feet and tried to defend himself, tried to escape, tried to fight, but William did nothing. He had nothing left worth defending, nowhere to escape to, and nothing worth fighting for.

William simply hung his head down and remembered their honeymoon on the cabin beside Lake Pleasant. He thought about watching the fish swirl through the reeds as they paddled across the water in a small rowing boat. He thought about the symphony of chirping birds, which woke them on their first day as husband and wife, about the smell of her perfume as it mingled with the pollen in the air. He thought about the feeling of holding her hand and feeling like nothing could pry them from one another. He thought about sitting on the edge of the jetty beside Abigale as they gently waded their feet through the water and watched the sun set. He remembered the view of the sun's pale pillar reflection as it stretched across the water's surface, and he remembered how it didn't hold a candle to the view of looking into his wife's emerald eyes as the amber sun danced through them. William and Abigale Lee were never as happy as they were by that lake, and they never would be again.

William was far too consumed by grief to notice the small primrose by her hand, or the peaceful look Cavanaugh had noticed in her eyes. Maybe it would've given him solace to see her calm gaze, maybe it would've given him a hint of the peace he would soon find. But even in this moment, his last moment with her, he still couldn't see Abigale in the way she always wanted him too. Such is the tragedy of Abigale Lee, even in a story as dark as this one, its darkest chapter is undoubtably its first.

William desperately wanted to stop the moments from passing, to hold himself in his memories with her for as long as possible before he truly realised she was gone. Sadly, the world didn't stop simply because William willed it to. His reminiscing soon cut to black as he was struck in the head by the butt of a rifle. The same rifle that would soon kill him. Such is life—circular, poetic, fleeting.

Printed and bound by CPI Group (UK) Ltd, Croydon, CR0 4YY